HOSTAGE!

Jessica hurried up the porch steps and leaned over the small railing to look into the living room window.

She wasn't certain exactly what she expected to see. But she almost gasped in surprise when she saw Mr. and Mrs. Morrow, right there in the kidnappers' living room.

Mrs. Morrow jumped to her feet the minute she saw Jessica's face in the window. "Wait!" Jessica mouthed at her, but the next instant Mrs. Morrow was pulling her husband out of sight.

Just then Jessica heard a footstep behind her. "What are you staring at?" a cross voice demanded.

Bantam Books in the Sweet Valley High Series
Ask your bookseller for the books you have missed

#1 DOUBLE LOVE
#2 SECRETS
#3 PLAYING WITH FIRE
#4 POWER PLAY
#5 ALL NIGHT LONG
#6 DANGEROUS LOVE
#7 DEAR SISTER
#8 HEARTBREAKER
#9 RACING HEARTS
#10 WRONG KIND OF GIRL
#11 TOO GOOD TO BE TRUE
#12 WHEN LOVE DIES
#13 KIDNAPPED!
#14 DECEPTIONS
#15 PROMISES
#16 RAGS TO RICHES
#17 LOVE LETTERS
#18 HEAD OVER HEELS
#19 SHOWDOWN
#20 CRASH LANDING!
#21 RUNAWAY
#22 TOO MUCH IN LOVE
#23 SAY GOODBYE
#24 MEMORIES
#25 NOWHERE TO RUN
#26 HOSTAGE!
#27 LOVESTRUCK
#28 ALONE IN THE CROWD
#29 BITTER RIVAL
#30 JEALOUS LIES
#31 TAKING SIDES
#32 THE NEW JESSICA

Super Edition: PERFECT SUMMER
Super Edition: SPECIAL CHRISTMAS
Super Edition: SPRING BREAK
Super Edition: MALIBU SUMMER

SWEET VALLEY HIGH

HOSTAGE!

Written by
Kate William
Created by
FRANCINE PASCAL

BANTAM BOOKS
TORONTO • NEW YORK • LONDON • SYDNEY • AUCKLAND

RL6, IL age 12 and up

HOSTAGE!

A Bantam Book / February 1986
4 printings through December 1986

Conceived by Francine Pascal.

Produced by Cloverdale Press, Inc.

Cover art by James Mathewuse.

ISBN 0-553-26749-3

Published simultaneously in the United States and Canada

Bantam Books are published by Bantam Books, Inc. Its trademark, consisting of the words "Bantam Books" and the portrayal of a rooster, is Registered in U.S. Patent and Trademark Office and in other countries. Marca Registrada. Bantam Books, Inc., 666 Fifth Avenue, New York, New York 10103.

PRINTED IN THE UNITED STATES OF AMERICA

O 13 12 11 10 9 8 7 6 5 4

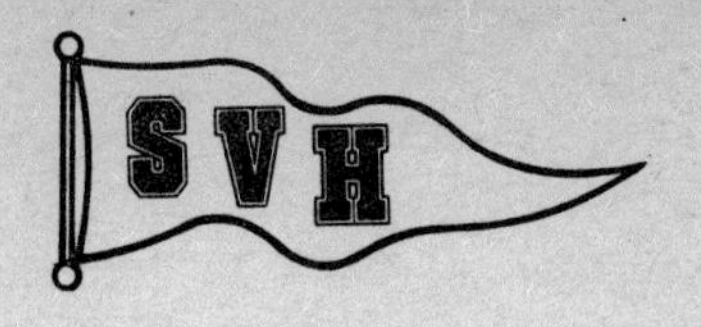

One

"I don't care what you say, Jessica," Elizabeth Wakefield protested, her aquamarine eyes darkening with concern. "I think something peculiar is going on over at the Morrows' house. And whatever it is, I just want to make sure Regina Morrow isn't in trouble!"

Elizabeth and Jessica Wakefield were stretched out on beach towels on the white pavement encircling the pool in the Wakefields' backyard, the late afternoon sun still warm on their backs. The twins were enjoying a rare hour of total relaxation between school and dinner, catching up on the events of the past week. It felt as if so much had happened that they hadn't been able to share lately! Partly that was because the twins' grandparents had just left Sweet Valley after a three-week visit. Moreover, lately Jessica had been putting in more hours with the cheerleading squad, and Elizabeth had been hard at work on an article for Sweet Valley High's student newspaper, *The Oracle*.

Jessica sat up on her towel, tossing her golden hair off her shoulders. From the expression on her face, it was clear that Jessica thought Elizabeth was jumping to conclusions about the strange woman who'd answered the door on Saturday at the Morrow estate. "I still don't get it," she said at last. "Why do you and Bruce think Regina's in trouble? Maybe Regina just doesn't want to see Bruce," she suggested mischievously, reaching past her twin for the bottle of baby oil on the lawn. "The poor girl's been through enough lately without having to face Bruce Patman the minute she's back in Sweet Valley!"

Elizabeth laughed. There was no love lost between Bruce Patman and her extremely opinionated twin sister Jessica. Elizabeth could remember when Jessica had felt differently about the handsome, but conceited, senior. In fact, Jessica had fallen hard for the wealthy Bruce Patman. But he had treated her badly, and Jessica, who wasn't used to being given a hard time, had retaliated. From then on it had been open war between those two.

Thinking about it, Elizabeth shook her head. She and her twin certainly responded differently.

In looks, the sixteen-year-old twins were mirror images, from their blond hair and wide-set, blue-green eyes to their slim, size-six figures. But their personalities and the ways they reacted to situations were not similar at all.

Elizabeth always tried to look and listen before she leaped. Thoughtful, dedicated, and hard-working, she had earned a reputation among the other juniors at Sweet Valley High as a good friend and a sympathetic listener. Jessica thought her sister was *too* thoughtful and dedicated. Not that Jessica didn't love her sister with all her heart, but Jessica was always looking for adventure. The fast lane appealed to her much more than the slow, cautious route. Jessica loved to tease her more serious sister, and from the expression on her face just then, it was obvious Jessica wasn't taking Elizabeth's concern over Regina Morrow seriously.

Regina was sixteen years old too, and in the junior class with the twins at Sweet Valley High. The Morrows had moved into the sumptuous estate in the most exclusive part of the Valley earlier that year, and Regina had quickly been accepted by her new classmates. Of course, Elizabeth reflected, it would be hard to imagine Regina *not* being well liked. Beautiful, soft-spoken and sweet-natured, the raven-haired girl had gone out of her way to be friendly. From the way she acted, you'd never guess she was the daughter of one of the wealthiest computer manufacturers on the West Coast or that she'd been approached by a local modeling agency soon after moving to Sweet Valley and had appeared on the cover of *Ingenue* magazine.

Most important, Elizabeth reflected, one couldn't tell Regina had a serious handicap. Years of training in a special school in Connecticut and work with private voice therapists made it almost impossible to tell that Regina had been born almost completely deaf.

For sixteen years Regina had lived in a world that was almost entirely silent. Her greatest aspiration, she'd confided in Elizabeth soon after the girls met, was to lead a normal life. But that wasn't easy. "When people find out I'm deaf, they back off," she'd continued shyly. And Elizabeth's heart had gone out to her.

Almost from the first, Elizabeth had felt protective of Regina. She could see why Nicholas, Regina's eighteen-year-old brother, got such a fierce look in his eyes whenever Regina seemed to be in a jam. The girl was so vulnerable! Elizabeth couldn't stand the thought of anything or anyone hurting her. That was why she'd been less than thrilled when Bruce Patman had started dating Regina. But as time went on, Elizabeth realized that Bruce had changed, and that he cared about Regina as much as she did.

Or more, Elizabeth corrected herself, remembering how selfless Bruce had been when he learned that a doctor in Switzerland had discovered a treatment that could restore Regina's hearing. The treatments were time-consuming and expensive. Worse, they had to be done where Dr. Friederich was—in Bern, Switzerland. Regina was faced with a terrible choice. Leave Bruce or lose the chance to regain her hearing.

For Regina it had been a deep conflict. If Bruce had interfered, who knew what she might have done? But by holding back, Bruce had allowed Regina to take Dr. Friederich up on his offer. For the past few months, she'd been in Switzerland, relying on frequent letters to stay in touch with her friends in Sweet Valley. Bruce heard from her at least once a week, usually more often, and Elizabeth had also received quite a few letters. She knew Regina was adjusting fairly well to her new home. Her private tutor was excellent, so she was keeping up with her studies and was hoping to be able to begin her senior year next fall with her classmates. Most important, the treatments were working. "I can't hear everything," her last letter to Elizabeth had reported, "but I'm definitely getting better. Some sounds are less distinct than others, but Dr. Friederich is convinced that eventually I'll have normal hearing. And the treatments are working much faster than he expected!"

But Regina hadn't said anything about leaving Switzerland. That was the strange thing. She hadn't written to Bruce about it either. So a few days before, when Eddie Strong reported that Regina was back in town,. Elizabeth had been surprised.

Eddie Strong was a sophomore who was working as a part-time delivery boy at the Thrift Mart, a twenty-four-hour supermarket in Sweet Valley. Elizabeth had run into him at the store when she was buying a carton of milk for her mother. And Eddie had asked if she'd seen Regina yet.

"Jessica, you have to listen to me!" Elizabeth said urgently, frowning as she remembered the chain of events that had led up to her hasty meeting with Bruce the day before. Assuming Regina had flown home for a surprise visit, Elizabeth had driven over to the Morrows' estate just to pop in and welcome her home. To her surprise, the gates at the end of the long driveway had been locked. Apparently no one was home; the place looked deserted.

Her next step had been to consult Bruce. If Regina really were back, Bruce would surely know about it, Elizabeth had reasoned. But Bruce had looked completely blank. As far as he knew, Regina was in Switzerland. He thought Eddie Strong had been mistaken.

Just to be sure, Bruce had phoned the Morrows. A strange woman had answered the phone. She said Regina was sleeping and the rest of the Morrows were away. And when Bruce asked her who she was, she said she was Regina's aunt. But Bruce knew that both of Regina's parents were only children.

Jessica looked at her twin as if she'd gone mad.

"I'm listening, I'm listening. But I still don't see what—"

"Look," Elizabeth cried. "Eddie went over to the Morrows' to make a delivery, right? And he saw Regina there. But *nobody else* knew she was in town. She didn't write anyone about it! And when I drove over there, the whole place was locked up. Then Bruce called, and some woman lied to him about who she was! It's creepy," she concluded as she remembered the way the Morrows' house had looked behind those locked gates.

"You're getting a Nancy Drew complex, that's what I think," Jessica said critically, frowning up at the sun. She giggled suddenly. "Only I can hardly imagine Bruce as Ned Nickerson!"

"Jess," Elizabeth said, "suppose Regina really is in some kind of trouble. Suppose—"

"Suppose the sun doesn't set tonight," Jessica said. "Maybe that way I can get some color again. My tan's completely faded."

"You're heartless." Elizabeth sighed. "Completely heartless. Regina may be trapped inside her own home by some maniac, and all you can think about is keeping your tan up!"

Elizabeth remembered the agony she'd been through several months before, when she had been kidnapped by an orderly who worked at Joshua Fowler Memorial Hospital, where she and Jessica had been working as volunteers. The orderly was named Carl, and it turned out that he was mentally disturbed. He had never intended to hurt Elizabeth; he just wanted to keep her with him forever.

All the same, the two days she had spent tied up in Carl's ramshackle house were the worst of Elizabeth's life. It made her stomach feel weak even to think of them now. Thank heavens she'd been rescued! If Regina were in the same kind of trouble . . .

Jessica seemed to be reading her mind. "Liz," she said patiently, "Regina is not bound and gagged in her own bedroom. I know what you're thinking. You're remembering Carl, aren't you? But this isn't the same thing at all, Liz. There's probably a perfectly logical explanation for all of this. Maybe Bruce is losing *his* hearing," she added, inspired. "Maybe she didn't say 'aunt' at all. Or maybe she's a cousin who just calls herself an aunt."

"Well . . ." Elizabeth said dubiously. She laughed suddenly, a thought occurring to her. "For once, *you're* trying to convince me to slow down and be rational. Do you think we're changing personalities?"

"I hope not." Jessica groaned. "I think," she added, "that all of this is Bruce's fault. Didn't you say his parents have gone away?"

Elizabeth nodded. "They're in Boston, I think. Why?"

"Well, Bruce is probably going a bit soft in the

head from being alone, that's all. He's the one who's planting crazy ideas in your head."

Elizabeth laughed. Jessica still wasn't tired of picking on Bruce Patman. All the same, Elizabeth didn't share her sister's lighthearted attitude toward what she suspected was going on at the Morrows' estate.

Not one to get excited or alarmed easily, Elizabeth found it almost impossible to suppress her concern once it had been aroused. She really did think something peculiar was happening, and she felt a chill creeping up her spine as she tried to put all the pieces together. She didn't care what Jessica thought. Something strange was going on, and she intended to do something about it!

"Where are you going?" Jessica demanded, her eyes widening as her twin jumped to her feet.

"I'm going to call Bruce," Elizabeth called over her shoulder as she hurried toward the sliding glass door at the back of the Wakefields' split-level house.

She had already decided what she was going to do as she dialed the Patmans' number on the phone in the study. Her eyes were still adjusting to the dim light inside when Bruce answered the phone.

"Elizabeth!" he said. "What's up?"

"I've been thinking constantly about what happened yesterday," Elizabeth confided, dropping her voice a little. "And I just wanted to let you know that I can't stand sitting around anymore."

"I know what you mean," Bruce agreed. "I'd pretty much decided the same thing myself. What do you think we should do?"

"Well, to begin with," Elizabeth told him, "I'm going over to the Morrows' again to have another look around. I keep thinking about the gates being locked, and it's bugging me. I just want to see what the place looks like again before we decide what to do."

"Why don't you let me meet you over there?" Bruce asked. "The whole thing scares me, Liz. I'd feel better if you weren't alone."

"Don't worry," Elizabeth assured him, her heart beginning to pound despite the confidence in her voice. "I'll be fine—and it'll be easier to sneak around and do some detective work by myself."

"Well . . ." Bruce said doubtfully. "When are you going to go?"

"Right now," Elizabeth said with sudden determination. "I don't see any point in waiting a minute longer. The sooner I get over there, the sooner we'll know exactly what's going on!"

"Just be careful," Bruce said seriously. "And call me when you get back. I've got a centennial meeting in half an hour, but I should be back around dinner time. OK?"

"OK," Elizabeth said, replacing the receiver on the hook after she'd said goodbye.

That was when she realized her fingers were trembling. For the first time since she'd begun to worry about Regina, Elizabeth admitted the truth to herself. She wasn't just worried anymore. She was frightened!

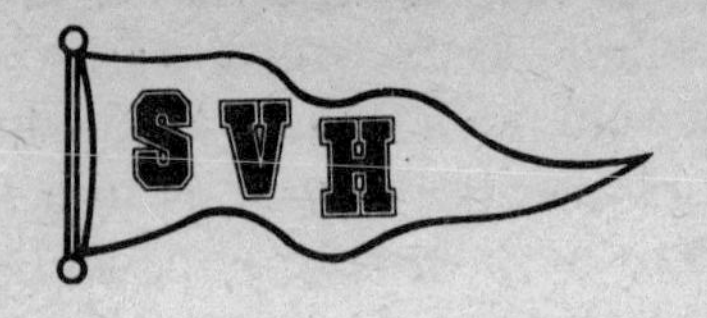

Two

The last light of afternoon was fading as Elizabeth drove through the winding streets leading up to the hill, the most exclusive part of Sweet Valley. Turning on the radio and humming along to keep up her courage, Elizabeth noticed that her hands were slipping on the steering wheel of the red Fiat Spider she and Jessica shared. She barely noticed the dappled shade trees overhead or the spectacular glimpses of the sapphire-colored ocean as the Fiat inched its way uphill. All she could think about was what she might find up ahead.

Her nervousness increased as she approached the Morrow estate. She could feel her heart begin to pound as the Fiat rounded the corner of the road and the estate suddenly loomed into view. "The gates are open!" Elizabeth exclaimed aloud, braking at the foot of the long driveway leading up to the main house. After a minute's hesitation, she touched her foot to the gas pedal again. "No time like the present for solving mysteries," she told herself, turning the Fiat into the Morrows' drive. Her heart pounding loudly, Elizabeth drove up the drive, parking at the top of the circular driveway as close as possible to the Morrows' front door.

Maybe it was just because she was nervous but the estate looked spooky that afternoon. Ordinarily Elizabeth loved the Morrows' mansion. Despite its size and grandeur, there was something welcoming, almost homey, about the place. Cypress trees, bushes, and flowers lined the walkway to the front doors. Today, Elizabeth noticed, the flowers looked uncared for, almost straggly.

Well, here goes nothing, Elizabeth thought, pressing the door bell. Remembering Jessica's skepticism, she felt a bit embarrassed by the way she was acting. *Jess would* really *think I was being a moron if she could see me trembling out here on the doorstep,* she thought.

But just then the door opened. A stern-faced woman stood there, looking Elizabeth over from head to foot. "Can I help you?" the woman asked coldly.

Elizabeth gulped. "I'm a classmate of Regina's," she said, trying to get a good look over the woman's shoulder at the Morrows' front hallway. "I mean, I *used* to be a classmate of hers before she went to Switzerland. I heard she was back in town for a visit, so I thought I'd just drop by and—"

"Regina isn't here," the woman snapped, starting to close the door. She had a tense, nervous expression on her face. Using her reporter's skills, Elizabeth tried to absorb as many details as possible about her. She wondered if this was the woman who told Bruce she was Regina's aunt. The woman appeared to be in her middle to late thirties. She had gray-streaked auburn hair and pale skin. But her eyes were her most unusual feature—gray and slightly slanted, with an expression that made Elizabeth shudder.

"Are you sure she isn't here?" Elizabeth asked again, her confidence returning. "I'm sure I heard that—" Suddenly her voice failed her. To her surprise, Regina had entered the foyer!

"Regina!" Elizabeth cried, waving at the raven-haired girl. "When did you get home? Bruce and I have been trying—"

A strange expression came over the woman's face as she turned and regarded Regina. "I thought I told you to stay upstairs," she said to Regina, her voice low and harsh. Regina stared helplessly out the front door at Elizabeth, her blue eyes burning with an urgency Elizabeth couldn't interpret. Regina stood frozen in the foyer for almost a minute. Then, a look of utter helplessness on her face, she turned in the direction of the stairway.

The woman appeared to be struggling to keep

her expression normal as she faced Elizabeth again. "Regina hasn't been feeling well," she said quickly, starting to close the front door. But Elizabeth had her foot in the way. "She can't see anyone right now. She isn't well," the woman repeated, an angry flush beginning to creep across her face.

Elizabeth ignored her. She had tried frantically to signal to Regina with her hands, but either Regina hadn't wanted to signal back or she was afraid to. In any case, the look on her face had said more than anything else could. She looked so helpless—and so alone. Elizabeth couldn't stand the thought of leaving her alone with the severe-looking woman in the doorway. But it didn't appear that she had much choice.

Without another word, the woman succeeded in forcing the door closed, and Elizabeth was left alone outside, staring helplessly at the heavy door, Regina locked in behind it.

Regina's image was vivid in Elizabeth's mind as she opened the door of the Fiat and slid into the driver's seat. Regina looked so—so vulnerable, Elizabeth thought. And so confused.

Elizabeth was more convinced than ever that something terrible was going on, but it still didn't make sense to her. Was that strange woman masquerading as Regina's aunt? And why? Was Regina being held in her very own house against her will?

Elizabeth felt almost dizzy with confusion and

alarm as she edged the Fiat around the curves leading down the big hill. Every question she could think of just led to a dozen more. Where were the Morrows, for example? And Nicholas? Did they even know the strange "aunt," or were they in trouble, too?

Elizabeth had no answers as she maneuvered the Fiat up the Wakefields' driveway. Her father's car was in the driveway ahead of her. A quick glance at her wristwatch told Elizabeth that it was already six-thirty.

The minute Elizabeth saw her father's car she made a quick decision. Mr. Wakefield was a lawyer, and Elizabeth had no doubt that he'd have some strong suggestions to make if she and Jessica told him about the strange sequence of events at the Morrow estate. Mr. Wakefield was a loving, protective father, and he'd want the twins to stay far away from trouble.

"Jess and I are going to have to keep this a secret!" Elizabeth told herself grimly, hurrying for the front door.

She wanted to get to her twin before Jessica could say anything to their parents about Regina. Otherwise, she had a feeling they'd both be barred from trying to help their friend. Their parents would never let them get involved in anything dangerous.

And after this afternoon, Elizabeth was certain that whatever was going on at the Morrows', investigating it wasn't going to be free of danger.

* * *

"Of course I didn't say anything to Daddy," Jessica said, frowning at her twin. She was lying on her side on the carpeted floor of her bedroom, lifting one leg in time to the aerobics record playing on her stereo.

Elizabeth looked around her. "From one messy situation to another!" She laughed and sank down on the only corner of Jessica's bed that wasn't piled with clothing. Jessica's room was a standing joke in the Wakefield household. From the brown walls to the tangle of clothing everywhere the eye could see, her room looked "lived in" on its best days. That day it looked like a federal disaster area.

"So what did you see over there?" Jessica prompted, sitting up and bouncing her blond head over to touch her knees.

"You know, it hurts just to watch you do that," Elizabeth commented. "How can I possibly tell you what I saw over at the Morrows' place while you're hanging upside down?"

"OK, OK," Jessica said, looking attentive at last. "Shoot."

Elizabeth shuddered. "I don't think I like that word right now, Jess. It gives me the creeps. As a matter of fact, almost everything is giving me the creeps today!"

"You must've stopped off to see Bruce," Jessica suggested, her aqua eyes twinkling.

"This is serious," Elizabeth said in a low voice. Standing, she walked over to the door and closed it, then sat down again on the bed. "That's why I don't want Mom or Dad finding out about it, Jess. They'd never let either of us go over there again if they thought something dangerous were going on."

"Liz, would you just get to the point and tell me what you saw?"

Elizabeth quickly filled her sister in on the strange woman who'd lied to her about Regina being home. "But Regina *was* there," she concluded. "I saw her in the foyer. And her expression was so odd when she looked at me, Jess—sort of imploring and frightened."

"I still think you've been reading too many thrillers," Jessica said after a minute's reflection. "But I have to admit, it sounds kind of weird. Do you think this woman is holding Regina hostage or something?"

"I think," Elizabeth said thoughtfully, "that it's too complicated now for us to deal with on our own."

"But you said you don't want Mom or Dad finding out!"

"I don't," Elizabeth said grimly. "But they're not exactly the people I had in mind. Jessica, I think we should call the police."

Jessica blinked. "Are you sure?" she asked dubiously. "Liz, don't you think you may be getting a little bit ahead of yourself? What if that lady really is Regina's aunt and she was just really grouchy this afternoon?"

"That's a chance we'll just have to take," Elizabeth said grimly, reaching for the extension on her sister's night table. "At this point, Jess, I'd rather be safe than sorry. And I think I'd feel a whole lot safer if the Sweet Valley Police Department were in on this!"

"What a day." Alice Wakefield sighed as she brought a platter of chicken to the dining room table. "I think I'll go crazy if I ever see another wallpaper pattern!" Slim, attractive and blond-haired, Mrs. Wakefield worked as an interior designer. Her blue eyes twinkled now as she filled her family in on the latest struggles with a particularly difficult client.

"Sounds like your day was sort of like mine," Ned Wakefield said, leaning back in his chair and grinning. Running his hand through his wavy, dark hair, he said, "This has been one of those weeks when I wonder if I shouldn't give up the law and head for the beach!"

"That sounds like a great idea, Daddy," Jessica said mischievously, reaching for the salad bowl. "We could sell the house and turn into nomads."

Elizabeth groaned. "Can you imagine Jessica being a nomad? She'd bring about thirty suitcases just filled with things for her hair!"

Just then the telephone rang, and the twins

exchanged nervous glances. Elizabeth had asked Sergeant O'Brien to call her back after he'd checked out the Morrow estate. That was probably him phoning back now.

"I'll get it!" both twins said in unison, jumping up and almost knocking each other over in the scramble for the kitchen phone. Elizabeth was half a second quicker and managed to lift the receiver before her sister. As she'd guessed, it was the police department calling. Sergeant O'Brien didn't sound very happy when he asked to speak to her.

Jessica was standing beside her, so Elizabeth moved the receiver a short distance away from her ear, so they could both hear what Sergeant O'Brien had to say.

"We made the check on the Morrow place, just like you asked us to," he said tersely. "But I couldn't find a single thing out of place. The woman who answered the door identified herself as Claire Davis, Skye Morrow's stepsister. She says she's visiting from out of town. Regina was upstairs when we stopped by, and we had no reason to think anything was wrong."

"I see," Elizabeth said weakly. Stepsister! That was a new twist. She and Bruce hadn't thought of that. She wanted to ask him if the Morrows themselves were around, but she was afraid to say anything with her parents listening. "Well, thank you very much," she added lamely.

"No problem," Sergeant O'Brien said shortly.

"Only next time," he added, "try not to get so alarmed just because your girlfriend isn't able to come outside and meet you. OK?"

Elizabeth shrugged her shoulders and looked helplessly at her sister as she replaced the receiver on the hook. *Great,* she thought miserably. *Now I've really done it!*

"Who was that?" Mrs. Wakefield asked as the twins walked back into the dining room.

"Oh, that was just someone with some information I was waiting for," Elizabeth said, resuming her seat. Her mother didn't question her, since Elizabeth was often gathering information for *Oracle* articles.

"Are you OK, honey?" Mrs. Wakefield asked a minute later, looking at Elizabeth with concern.

"I'm fine," Elizabeth murmured. She had been staring off into space. She forced herself to eat a bite of salad, but she could barely taste her mother's delicious blue-cheese dressing.

Bruce had said that Mrs. Morrow didn't have a sister, she thought. But did she have a stepsister? If not, who could Claire Davis be?

Elizabeth could tell Sergeant O'Brien had been trying to give her a message: *Butt out. Whatever's going on over there, it's none of your business!* But Elizabeth couldn't forget the image of Regina Morrow standing in the hallway, her blue eyes wide with fear.

I've got to do something, Elizabeth thought desperately. *If there's the slightest possibility that*

Regina is in danger, I've got to do everything I can to help her.

She didn't care what Sergeant O'Brien thought. She was going to call Bruce the minute dinner was over. She wouldn't be satisfied till she was certain they'd done everything they could to make sure Regina wasn't in danger.

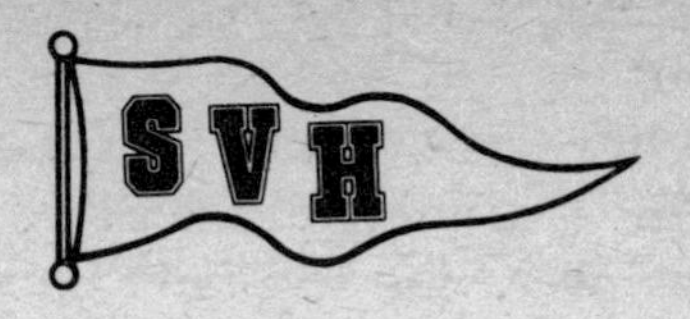

Three

"Liz, I've got to talk to you!" Jessica sang out, hurrying up the stairs after her twin.

"Why?" Elizabeth asked, her eyes narrowing as she turned to face her sister. "You just want to hear what the police said so you can tease me again about Nancy Drew."

Jessica shook her head. "No!" she objected. "I was thinking about Regina during dinner. And I think you're absolutely right. Something weird has *got* to be going on!"

Elizabeth blinked. "Well, the police department doesn't think so. Sergeant O'Brien sounded like he wanted to drag me down to the station and rap me on the knuckles. They probably think I get a kick out of making crank complaints!"

Jessica snorted. "They don't know anything," she said mysteriously, grabbing her sister's arm and pulling her up the remaining stairs. "Come on," she hissed. "Let's go to your room. We've got to talk about this alone."

Elizabeth shook her head. Jessica was famous for throwing herself headlong into things. From the expression on her face, it looked as if what was happening at the Morrows' was going to be her latest obsession.

"I've figured out how we can get through to Regina and find out what's going on over there!" Jessica exclaimed, whirling around to face Elizabeth after closing the door behind her. "Liz, I've come up with the perfect scheme. You're going to kick yourself for not having thought of it ages ago!"

"Go on." Elizabeth threw herself across her bed. "Tell me your plan, Sherlock Holmes. I'm all ears."

"Eddie Strong," Jessica said, folding her arms and looking at her sister with obvious satisfaction. "You forgot all about him, didn't you?"

Elizabeth frowned. "I don't get it. What good is Eddie going to do us now?"

Jessica looked as though she couldn't believe her own ears. "My own sister," she said mournfully, "doesn't even know the first thing about solving mysteries! But that's where you're lucky." She giggled. "Remember all those times at the beach when you were reading some big boring novel and I was reading Agatha Christie? It's paying off now!"

"Spare me," Elizabeth said, laughing. "Just tell me what your ace-sleuth mind has in store for poor Eddie Strong."

"Well, it's perfectly simple," Jessica said airily. "Eddie made a delivery to the Morrows last week, right?"

"Right," Elizabeth confirmed. "Or for this Claire Davis woman, anyway. We don't really know where the Morrows are."

"That doesn't matter now," Jessica said reprovingly. "What matters is getting some kind of message to Regina. And *that's* where Eddie comes in."

Elizabeth's eyes widened. "You mean use Eddie to—"

"I mean," Jessica interrupted, "finding out from Eddie when the next delivery is supposed to be made to the Morrows'. Then we'll ask him if we can make the delivery for him. That way," she added, her eyes flashing, "we can sneak a message in for Regina. How's that for master sleuthing?"

"Jessica Wakefield, you're a genius!" Elizabeth cried, jumping up and throwing her arms around her twin. "But who's going to pretend to be the delivery boy?" she asked a second later.

"Bruce, obviously," Jessica answered. "That'll be some sight!"

"OK," Elizabeth said, thinking fast. "Why don't you call Eddie, and I'll call Bruce. Find out when he's supposed to take this week's delivery over, and make sure it won't cause a problem if we make the delivery for him. OK?"

"OK," Jessica said, her expression suddenly turning solemn. "Liz, do you think Regina's really in serious trouble?"

Elizabeth bit her lip. "I don't know," she said nervously. "But I'm really glad you're willing to help now, Jess. Because if she is in trouble, Bruce and I are going to need all the help we can get!"

"Wait a minute," Bruce said anxiously. "Liz, you're going so fast I can't keep up with you! Now tell me what happened again from the minute that woman opened the Morrows' front door."

Elizabeth was on the extension in her bedroom, trying to keep her voice down in case her parents came upstairs. "She was really strange, Bruce," she told him, shuddering again as she remembered Claire Davis's steely gray eyes. "And she wouldn't let me in! She kept trying to shut the door on me. That was when I saw Regina," she added.

Bruce's voice was choked with emotion. "How did she look, Liz? Was she OK? If that woman's trying to hurt her—if *anyone* tries to hurt her . . ."

"She looked fine," Elizabeth said gently.

"Bruce, are you absolutely sure that neither of Regina's parents has a stepsister? Because the policeman said that—"

"She's lying!" Bruce broke in, angry and upset. "I don't know who that woman is, but I know she's lying! Regina's parents are both only children. And neither of them have stepsisters!"

"Bruce," Elizabeth whispered, looking nervously at her closed door, "try not to get upset. I know how you must be feeling, but if we're going to help Regina—"

"There's no 'if' about it," Bruce cut in. "Liz, we've got to do something—right away!"

"You're right," Elizabeth told him. "I couldn't agree more." And taking a deep breath, she outlined Jessica's scheme. "Jess is downstairs, calling Eddie Strong on the second line that our parents just had installed," she added. "As soon as she finds out when the next delivery is supposed to be made, we can set a time to meet."

"It better be soon," Bruce said grimly. "I can't stand the thought of Regina trapped over there with some strange woman for very much longer."

"Are you all right?" Elizabeth asked him, concerned. Something about his voice worried her. She could imagine how frustrating it must be for him, wondering whether or not Regina was in danger.

"Yeah," Bruce said and sighed. "I'm fine. Just a little tired, that's all. I got dragged into a meeting with Coach Schultz and Mr. Collins today. Mr. Collins was really laying into Ken Matthews."

Elizabeth was surprised. Blond, good-looking Ken was captain of the football team and one of the most popular boys in the junior class, and Mr. Collins was a very fair teacher. "What was the problem?"

Bruce didn't sound very interested in Ken just then. "Ken is flunking English," he muttered. "His grades are so bad that he might not be able to stay on the football team. And the coach is all upset because there's that big centennial game coming up against Palisades High. Anyway, it turned into a big free-for-all. I got dragged into the discussion because I'm head of the student centennial committee. The game is a really big part of the whole thing, and without Ken on the team, we won't stand a chance against Palisades."

"That's too bad," Elizabeth said. She knew Ken had Mr. Collins for English, and she was surprised Ken was doing so badly. Mr. Collins was a wonderful teacher, and all the students liked him, Ken included. And it must be killing Ken to be faced with having to quit the team. But at Sweet Valley the rule was that no student could participate in extracurricular activities without passing grades in all subjects.

It sounded as though Bruce had his hands full. Sweet Valley had been planning its centennial celebration for some time. Elizabeth knew how much it meant to Bruce to do a good job representing the high school in the civic celebration. The game against Palisades High was one of the biggest events in the celebration, and obviously Bruce wanted it to go smoothly.

"What do you think Ken's problem is?" Elizabeth asked. "It isn't like him to be having trouble—and I thought he really liked English!"

"Everyone likes English," Bruce said gloomily. "Even I did—until about three o'clock this afternoon. Now I feel like it's making my life even more complicated than it already is."

Elizabeth was quiet for a minute. She knew Mr. Collins better than many of her classmates because he was the faculty adviser to *The Oracle*. Elizabeth liked him a lot, and she was sure that whatever was going on with Ken, Mr. Collins would help straighten it out.

But Elizabeth's train of thought was interrupted as Jessica pushed the door open and hurried over, her face flushed and her eyes shining. "Tell Bruce we're in business," Jessica declared. "I just talked to Eddie Strong, and he's supposed to make a delivery at the Morrows' place tomorrow afternoon!"

Elizabeth felt a chill creeping up her spine. They were really going to do it! There was no turning back now.

"Bruce," she said into the receiver, "Jessica's

cleared everything with Eddie. And it looks like we're on for tomorrow after school. Are you ready to masquerade as a delivery boy?"

"Ready!" Bruce exclaimed, his voice cracking with emotion. "Elizabeth Wakefield, you've got yourself a date!"

"Just run it by me one more time," Elizabeth said. She was sitting on Jessica's bed in her nightshirt, uneasily scanning the letter she and Jessica had written to Regina on a sheet of notebook paper. "Dear Regina," the letter began.

> We know you're home, and we're worried about you. Are you OK? If you can, write us a note. If you wrap it around something heavy and drop it out your window, we can pick it up tonight. Tell us everything you can in the letter—what we can do to help and who we should go to.
>
> And promise us you'll be careful!
>
> Love,
>
> Bruce, Elizabeth, and Jessica

"What do we do with it?" Elizabeth continued. "How can we make sure Regina will get it and Claire Davis won't?"

Jessica bounced up from her desk. "I already thought of that," she said triumphantly. "The object is to think of something from the store for Regina and tuck the letter inside. Eddie says the Morrows have a standing order at the store—eggs, milk, butter, things like that. If we include something extra, it'll catch Regina's eye. And the best thing I can think of," she finished off, "is a copy of *Ingenue* magazine. Thrift Mart carries magazines, and from the way you've described Claire Davis, *she* won't be interested in fashion or beauty!"

"You've outdone yourself." Elizabeth chuckled. "So what do we do while Bruce is dropping off the groceries?"

"We hide out," Jessica said solemnly. "We'll be covering him, you see, to make sure no one comes and captures the getaway car while he's making the delivery."

"It's like being in a James Bond movie!" Elizabeth exclaimed.

"Our biggest job is going to be hiding the car, come to think of it," Jessica remarked.

"Why?" Elizabeth demanded.

Jessica dissolved into a fit of giggles. "Have you ever heard of a delivery boy driving around in a black Porsche?"

Elizabeth started to laugh too. But she had a feeling that underneath her merriment, Jessica was as scared as she was. This wasn't kid's stuff they were fooling around with. And Elizabeth had an uneasy suspicion they might be putting their necks on the line the minute they tried to help. But they had no choice. They'd just have to plunge ahead, no matter what. If they didn't save Regina, no one else would.

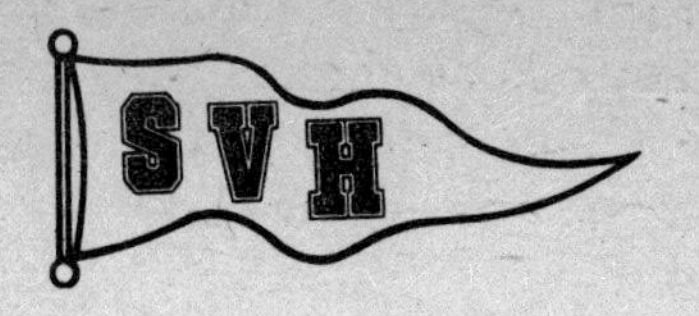

Four

It was Wednesday afternoon, and the twins were with Bruce in his black Porsche, driving to the Morrows'. Elizabeth was in the front, and Jessica sat in the back, a box of groceries on the seat beside her.

"Here we are," Bruce said, slowing the car down as he rounded the last curve before the Morrow estate. "Do you guys know exactly what to do if something goes wrong?"

"I think so," Elizabeth said uneasily. "Jess and I are going to stay with the car just out of sight of the house while you drop off the groceries. If you run into any sort of trouble, you're going to whistle twice, and we'll drive over to your house and wait for you there."

Bruce turned the car down the Morrows' long driveway and stopped about fifty yards from the mansion. He expertly maneuvered the Porsche in a tight U-turn to face the road. "That should do it," he remarked. "I don't think anyone'll be able to see the car from the house. Here are the keys," he added, handing them to Elizabeth. "And remember, if you hear me whistle, *don't wait*. Just take off! And," he added darkly, "if I don't show up back at my house in half an hour, call the police again and tell them there really *is* trouble up here."

Elizabeth swallowed as she watched the handsome, broad-shouldered senior walk toward the house, the box of groceries in his arms. "I hope he'll be all right," she whispered to Jessica.

"I hope so, too," Jessica said. "I have to admit, Bruce is pretty devoted to Regina," she added after a minute or two. "I'd never have believed it in a million years, but he's actually taking a risk for someone!"

Elizabeth nodded without saying a word. She felt a lump form in her throat as she watched Bruce disappear up the drive.

Elizabeth was trying her hardest to hide her anxiety, but secretly she was apprehensive about that afternoon's adventure. There were so many things that could go wrong! What if "Aunt Claire" didn't give Regina the magazine? Worse, what if Claire found the note they'd written? There was no telling what she might do to Regina if she knew Bruce and the twins were trying to get in touch with her!

It made Elizabeth's heart sink to think about it.

All she could do was stare down the long driveway, waiting for Bruce to come back into sight.

Jessica spotted him first. "There he is!" she cried. "Start the car up, Liz! It looks like he's running!"

Her heart pounding, Elizabeth fumbled with the metal ring as she tried to find the right one to fit in the ignition. At last she turned the motor on. Bruce was panting as he tore down the last stretch of road and yanked the car door open. Elizabeth scrambled over to the passenger side as Bruce hopped into the driver's seat.

"Are you all right?" the twins cried in unison.

Bruce pulled the gearshift into drive and pressed on the gas pedal. "I'm fine," he said tersely, shifting gears again and accelerating. "I dropped the groceries off," he continued, wiping his forehead with one hand. "A woman opened the door. She must be the same one you saw, Liz. About thirty-five, with grayish hair. She looked really mean."

"That's her!" Elizabeth cried. "That's Claire Davis."

"Well, she took the box from me and said thanks. Nothing else. I couldn't get a good look inside, but there wasn't anyone else around as far as I could tell." Bruce laughed. "She gave me fifty cents. I guess she isn't much of a tipper."

"Why were you running, then?" Jessica demanded. "We thought someone was chasing you!"

Bruce shrugged, his face reddening a little. "She was really weird. I just wanted to get away from her." His expression darkened. "Just thinking about that woman . . . if she's done anything to hurt Regina . . ."

"We'll just have to hope that Regina gets our note," Elizabeth said quietly. "What time should we meet you tonight, Bruce?"

"My parents are away, remember? Whenever you two can get away is fine with me."

"Why don't we meet at nine o'clock at your house?" Jessica suggested. "It'll be good and dark by then."

Elizabeth shuddered. Good and dark, she thought anxiously.

Who knew what they'd find waiting for them beneath Regina's window—a note from Regina or a surprise of some sort from the mysterious "Aunt Claire"?

Regina was sitting listlessly on her bed, tracing the flowers on her bedspread with her finger. Four o'clock, her alarm clock said. But Regina didn't care what time it was. Time seemed to have stopped from the minute she got out of the taxi at the airport in Bern eight days earlier.

She had gone to the airport to meet her parents, who had written saying that Mr. Morrow had some urgent business in Geneva and they would stop in Bern first to visit her. They had asked her to meet them at gate one in the main terminal at one-thirty, and Regina had been there, beside herself with excitement. She couldn't wait to see her parents and to show them how much better she was. Dr. Friederich was amazed by her progress. She could already distinguish almost all the words in conversations around her. She couldn't wait to be able to hear her parents speak!

She hadn't suspected anything was wrong until the woman was right next to her. The woman was alone. She put her hand on Regina's arm and looked Regina straight in the eyes. "I have a gun," she'd whispered. "It's in my bag, and I'm going to ask that you not make me use it. I want you to listen to me very carefully and do exactly what I say. That way there won't be any trouble."

"My parents . . ." Regina had faltered, backing off.

The woman had tightened her grip on Regina's forearm. "Let me introduce myself," she had whispered hoarsely. "I'm Claire. *Aunt* Claire. And I'm going to take you back to Sweet Valley with me this evening. But first we're going to go to your apartment to pack a bag and get your passport. You will phone your doctor and tell him that your parents want you to come back to Sweet Valley for a couple of weeks."

Regina couldn't believe this was really happening. It was like something on television—or some kind of terrible nightmare. "Where *are* my parents?" she had demanded.

Claire's eyes narrowed, her fingers digging hard into her arm. "Just do as I say," she said smoothly, pulling Regina forward, "and there won't be any trouble. Your parents are being held hostage," she added. "If you make things difficult, if you give me any trouble at all, your parents will be killed. Do you understand?"

Regina's eyes filled with tears now as she remembered Claire's words. How many times since that moment had she thought of trying to escape or trying to call the police? Each time, however, Claire's sickening words would come back to her. *"Your parents will be killed."* Regina had never felt so helpless in her entire life. She had to do everything Claire told her to do, no matter what. Her parents' lives depended on it!

Nicholas, Regina's eighteen-year-old brother, was the only one she knew for sure was safe. He was in San Francisco, visiting a friend named Buddy Ames. Her parents had written her in Bern, saying that he was taking a vacation while they were in Europe and was going to be spending a couple of weeks in San Francisco.

Regina still didn't know what was going on. When she and Claire had arrived at the Morrow estate, a thin, mean-looking man was waiting in the living room for them. He told Regina that her parents were safe but well hidden and they'd be fine as long as she cooperated. He hadn't told her much—just what he expected her to do.

Apparently her father's plant had just designed a microchip that would revolutionize the computer industry. Mr. Morrow had spent the better part of the past five years perfecting this chip and had just manufactured a single working prototype. It had been the crowning achievement of his work in the computer industry and had taken thousands of research hours and endless expense.

And this man wanted the prototype.

That was where Regina came in. Using Regina, he planned to get the chip prototype from the plant. He was going to force Mr. Morrow to call Walter Frank, the plant manager, and tell him that he was detained in Europe. He would then instruct Walter to give the chip to Regina when she showed up at the plant. This man would get the chip, and her father's business would be destroyed.

That was all Regina knew. She had no idea when the chip was supposed to be stolen. She hadn't been able to figure that out yet. She was almost beginning to wish it would happen soon. Living like this was unbearable. Whatever came next would *have* to be better, she thought.

At first Regina had been too frightened to think. Now the fear was wearing off a little, and she was getting angry. Really angry. She hated Claire and the strange man with all her heart.

She couldn't stand what they were doing to her and her parents. Why would anyone want to hurt them so badly? It made her sick to think about it.

A sharp knock on her door jerked Regina out of her reverie. "The delivery boy just came," Claire said, sticking her head in the door. "They put in a magazine by mistake." She threw the magazine unceremoniously on the bed, closing the door again without another word.

Regina sat perfectly still, staring down at the spot where the magazine had fallen. It *wasn't* her imagination. A square of paper had shaken loose when the magazine hit the bed. It was a piece of notebook paper, folded several times.

Picking it up with trembling fingers, Regina unfolded the paper and began to read.

"Well, that ought to do it," Regina said to herself that evening, folding the letter she'd written and quickly scanning her bedroom for something heavy to weight it with. Her eye fell on a silver compact on her dresser, and a minute later she had tucked the letter inside the compact. Opening the window, she leaned out into the darkness and dropped the compact onto the soft grass below. Now all she could do was wait—wait and pray that Bruce and the twins would be able to do something.

Despite her anxiety, Regina felt better knowing they were trying to help. If anyone could save her and her parents, she thought, it would be those three.

She just hoped they could—and soon. Because she had a terrible feeling that time was beginning to run out.

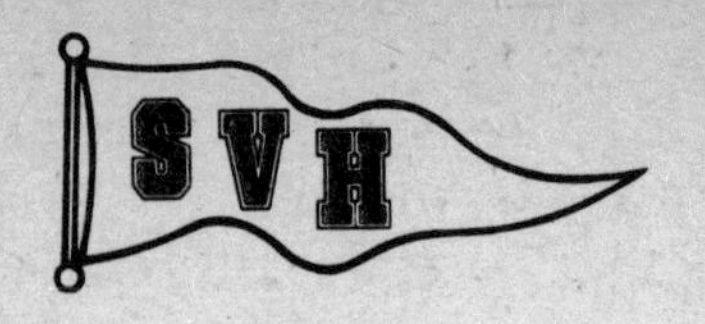

Five

"Liz!" Jessica exclaimed. "God, you scared me half to death," she hissed, dropping her voice. "I thought you were . . . I don't know who I thought you were!"

"Keep it down, you two," Bruce whispered hoarsely, turning the beam of his penlight over the damp grass.

"It's so dark out here," Jessica whispered. It was nine-thirty, and the three had climbed over the fence and crept stealthily across the grounds of the Morrow estate in the moonlit darkness. The twins' Fiat was hidden in a thicket of grass near the entrance to the estate.

"There isn't anything out here," Jessica said mournfully, rubbing her arms a little to warm herself up. "She must not have gotten our letter."

"Wait a minute!" Elizabeth cried excitedly. "There's something in the grass over by Bruce!"

Bruce dropped to his knees, searching the thick grass with his penlight. "Liz is right," he said, picking up the object. "It's Regina's compact, and there's a letter inside!"

"What's that?" Jessica said uneasily, cocking her head in the direction of the driveway. "Did either of you hear something, or am I just—"

"Shhh!" Elizabeth said warningly, listening hard. It did sound as though something was moving in the bushes, but the only sound she heard was the wind. "You're hearing things," she scolded Jessica.

"Let's not stick around, anyway," Bruce said, slipping the compact into his pocket and turning off his penlight. "Come on, you two, let's head for the car!"

The next thing she knew, Elizabeth was running behind Jessica and Bruce across the dewy grass.

Elizabeth had never run so fast in her life. Beside her she could hear Jessica panting as they raced across the dark lawn. It seemed as though they'd been running forever before they reached the wrought-iron fence surrounding the Morrows' property.

Bruce helped the twins get safely to the other side before pulling himself up and over the fence. "Let's get to the car!" he shouted. He rushed into the thicket, toward the Fiat.

Jessica brushed her hair back from her perspiring forehead as she crowded into the passenger seat of the sports car with Bruce. "I'm not so sure this is a good idea anymore," she gasped, her face flushed from exertion. "You guys, I don't like this. I think we've got to go back to the police!"

"We can't," Bruce said grimly. "Not unless we want to risk Regina's life—and her parents'."

"What are you talking about?" Elizabeth said, her eyes widening in horror.

Bruce had turned on his light and was reading the letter he'd found beneath Regina's window. "Take a look at this if you *really* want to get scared," he muttered, tossing the folded paper and penlight onto Elizabeth's lap.

Elizabeth read the letter as quickly as Jessica's interruptions would allow. In it Regina explained that she and her parents had all been kidnapped. So far, her parents were safe; the kidnappers had allowed them to write her a note. She outlined the plan to use her to steal the precious microchip from her father's plant. "They made my father call the servants and tell them all to take a vacation, but I don't know for how long," she went on.

"Please be careful," the letter continued. "These people are really dangerous. You've got to find out where they're holding my parents and rescue all three of us at the same time, or they'll kill whoever's left. They really will. And whatever you do, *don't call the police.* A patrol car came over the night before last, and 'Aunt Claire' was so mad she locked me in my room and threatened to tie me up and gag me."

"Oh, *no,*" Elizabeth groaned. "That was my fault!"

"Keep reading," Bruce said tersely.

Elizabeth cleared her throat and read the last part of the letter aloud. "Nicholas is staying with a friend of the family in San Francisco. His name is Buddy Ames, and he lives on Delaney Street. Please call him and let him know what's going on. Promise me you'll all be careful. I am so frightened. If I never see you again—"

"Stop!" Bruce groaned. "God, this is torture!"

"Where to now?" Jessica asked as Elizabeth started the Fiat.

"Back to Bruce's," Elizabeth answered grimly. "I want to get Buddy Ames's number right away. We've got to get Nicholas down from San Francisco to help us, and we haven't got a minute to lose!"

Fifteen minutes later Bruce had gotten through to Nicholas. "I don't want to scare you," he said in a low, controlled voice, "but you've got to get back to Sweet Valley as soon as you can. Is there any way you can get a flight down tonight?"

Nicholas sounded alarmed. "Tell me what's going on," he demanded. "Is it my parents? Has there been some kind of accident?"

"There's been some trouble," Bruce said evenly, "but they're OK, Nicholas. Everyone's

OK. But we need your help. I can't go into it on the phone," he added. "But the sooner you can get yourself back in town, the better I'm going to feel."

"I drove up, I didn't fly," Nicholas said grimly. "If I leave right now, I can be back in the Valley before breakfast."

"That's perfect," Bruce said, breathing a sigh of relief and giving the twins a thumbs-up sign. "One more thing," he added. "Come straight to my house when you get into town."

"What are you talking about?" Nicholas demanded. "Why can't I just go home?"

"It's a long story," Bruce said. He sighed heavily. "And one that I think will be easier to go into in person."

Elizabeth caught her sister's eye and shook her head. How in the world were they going to tell Nicholas that Regina was being held hostage in her own house and his parents were being held somewhere else—God only knew where!

Poor Nicholas, she thought sadly, trying to imagine how confused and apprehensive he must be right then.

"Well," Bruce said, replacing the receiver on the hook, "I guess we'd better call it a night. There isn't much else we can do before Nicholas gets here tomorrow."

Jessica looked up from Regina's letter, which she had been reading and rereading while Bruce was on the phone. "What do you suppose Claire meant by saying 'Money is heaven'?" she asked. "Regina says here that that's the only thing she couldn't make out when Claire was talking on the phone about when they were going to steal the chip. 'Money is heaven.' What could she possibly have meant by that?"

"It's probably a code," Elizabeth said. "She'd hardly just announce when the deal's supposed to be carried through with Regina standing around, would she?"

"If it is a code," Bruce said, "it may be our strongest clue so far—if we only knew how to crack it."

"Poor Regina," Elizabeth whispered, her face draining of color as she tried to imagine what her friend must be going through. "Bruce, do you really think we'll be able to help rescue the Morrows without any help from the police?"

"We've got to try," Bruce said, getting to his feet. "You read the note, Liz. You know we can't risk having another squad car show up."

"Bruce is right," Jessica said. "Regina's counting on us, Liz. We've got to come up with a plan to save her."

"Maybe Nicholas can help," Elizabeth said. "What time should we meet you tomorrow, Bruce?"

"Let's make it right after school," Bruce suggested. "I'm going to stay home tomorrow so I can let Nicholas know what's going on. Why don't you two come over here as soon as you can?"

Elizabeth and Jessica exchanged uneasy glances. "Tomorrow afternoon." Elizabeth sighed. "It feels like ages and ages away!"

Jessica looked anxious. "I'll have to skip cheerleading, but I guess if—"

Bruce silenced her with a look. "We're all going to have to skip things for a while. We're working against the clock."

Elizabeth had a terrible feeling he was right.

It was almost three thirty the next afternoon when Jessica and Elizabeth hurried through the Patmans' enormous mansion to the patio, where Bruce and Nicholas were sitting, two untouched glasses of iced tea on the table in front of them. The aqua water of the Patmans' Olympic-sized swimming pool glinted in the sunlight.

"Nicholas!" Elizabeth cried, running across the patio and throwing her arms around his neck. Nicholas and Elizabeth were special friends. For a while the dark-haired eighteen-year-old had been interested in something more than friendship, but the timing hadn't been right for Elizabeth. She was very fond of Nicholas, though, and she could tell from the look on his face that he was glad she was there.

"Nicholas knows the whole story," Bruce said, offering the twins chairs. "At least, as much of it as we know. He's seen Regina's letter."

"What I don't know," Nicholas said darkly, "is what kind of jerk would do something like this. It makes me so angry!" A shudder ran through him. "Bruce has been wonderful," he added quietly. "I wanted to go home and just punch this Claire in the face. And I would've, too, if Bruce hadn't held me down!"

Elizabeth and Jessica exchanged nervous glances.

"I'm so worried," Nicholas whispered. "First I think about Regina, trapped with some madwoman in that house. That's bad enough. Then I start to think about my parents, wondering where they are and if they're really OK . . ."

"I was just asking Nicholas if he could think of anyone who might be involved in this thing," Bruce told the twins. "I was wondering if his father has any enemies, anyone who would want to hurt him or his company."

Nicholas shook his head and ran a hand through his hair. "Everyone loves my father," he said brokenly.

Elizabeth took a deep breath. There didn't seem to be a clue to the kidnappers' identities.

"Look," Nicholas said, jumping to his feet. "I can't just sit around here anymore, Bruce. I appreciate how you feel, and, believe me, I don't want to risk hurting Regina, either. You know how I feel about her. But we've got to do something! I'm going to go and find out what's going on," he concluded, grabbing his jacket from the back of the chair.

"Nicholas, you can't!" Jessica wailed, her eyes darkening with fear. "Liz, tell him not to go!"

But Elizabeth knew Nicholas well enough to recognize his determination. "Jess, stay here with Bruce," she said quietly, getting to her feet. "If Nicholas wants to go check out the estate, I'm going with him."

Nicholas gave her a grateful look, a look that almost made up for the sinking feeling in her stomach.

There was no turning back now. Nicholas was already striding across the Patmans' lawn toward his Jeep, and Elizabeth had to run for a few yards to catch up with him. She could hear Bruce and Jessica calling after them, but following Nicholas's lead, Elizabeth didn't look back.

Before Nicholas got into the Jeep, Elizabeth stopped him, however. "Nicholas," she said breathlessly, "I think we'd better take my car. I wouldn't want to take a chance on anyone at the house seeing your Jeep—for your or Regina's sake."

"You're right, Liz," Nicholas said. "I guess I'm too upset to be thinking straight."

It took almost no time at all for Elizabeth to drive down the road to the Morrow estate. She had just stopped near the main gates when she and Nicholas noticed a blue car coming down the front drive.

Elizabeth felt as if she were going to faint. Whoever was in that car was liable to be curious about what she and Nicholas were doing there. What were they going to do now?

"I'm going to kiss you," Nicholas said suddenly, under his breath. "Try to act natural."

Elizabeth was too surprised to say a word. The next thing she knew, Nicholas had enfolded her in his arms, touching her lips gently with his own. The blue car did not pass them; she could tell by the sound of the motor that it had turned left and was speeding away from them.

Elizabeth breathed a sigh of relief as she pulled away from Nicholas. Nicholas's ruse had worked. If the driver of the blue car had noticed them, he must have assumed they were just a couple out for a romantic drive.

"Have you got a pen in your bag?" Nicholas demanded, breaking free and squinting at the tail end of the disappearing car. Elizabeth nodded, handing him a blue ballpoint.

"Did you get the license-plate number?" she asked, watching him scribble something down.

Nicholas nodded. "The weird thing is I caught a brief glimpse of him when he was coming down the driveway. He looks vaguely familiar, but I don't know why."

Elizabeth was too upset to respond to

Nicholas's remark. "Nicholas, I'm scared," she said. "Can't we go back to Bruce's now?"

Nicholas didn't answer. He was staring out the window, his brow furrowed with concentration. "OK, Liz," he said at last. "Just seeing this much has convinced me we'd better be awfully careful. I'd kill myself if my own carelessness were to bring any harm to Regina or my parents."

During the short drive back to the Patmans', Elizabeth and Nicholas talked about the contents of Regina's letter. Nicholas was convinced that their best bet was to try to figure out when "Aunt Claire" and her friend planned to take Regina to the plant. "Once they've got the chip," he said, "they're going to be out of here like a bolt of lightning. Liz, we've got to move fast."

Elizabeth agreed. "If only we knew what Regina overheard on the phone," she said. "Do you have any idea what 'money is heaven' could mean? Is it some kind of company password?"

Nicholas shook his head. "My father doesn't use passwords as far as I know."

By then they were back at the Patmans'. Elizabeth parked the car, and she and Nicholas walked around the mansion to the patio.

"How'd you make out?" Bruce asked when he caught sight of them. "Anything new?"

Nicholas shook his head. "We saw a car coming down the front drive, so we had to take cover fast. I got a quick look at the driver, though, and

I took down his license-plate number. He drives a beat-up blue Dodge."

"Maybe he's the one Regina wrote about in her note," Jessica said.

"Maybe he is," Nicholas responded. "The weird thing is he looks kind of familiar, but I can't remember how I know him."

"Jess and I were talking while you two were gone," Bruce said thoughtfully. "We've been trying to figure out who could possibly do this sort of thing to your dad and his family. Nicholas, are you absolutely sure that your father doesn't have any enemies? Someone he competed against in the computer business, perhaps?"

Nicholas looked thoughtful. "There was someone—a guy who worked for my dad in his Connecticut plant. But it was ages ago, maybe five years."

"Go on," Jessica prompted. "What happened with him?"

"He was a snake," Nicholas said. "I was pretty young, so I don't remember all the details, but I think he was caught stealing and my father had him arrested. That's right!" he said, snapping his fingers. "His name was Denson. Phillip Denson."

"So what happened to him?" Bruce demanded, leaning forward.

"Well, if I remember correctly, he was convicted," Nicholas said, thinking hard. "Wait a minute!" He snapped his fingers again. "He got out of prison last year and moved to California, I'm almost positive. I think I remember Dad saying something about it to the manager at the plant."

"Nicholas, what is it?" Elizabeth demanded. She'd never seen Nicholas look so fired-up before.

A hush fell over the table as Bruce leaned forward. "Was that Phillip Denson?" he whispered.

Nicholas nodded. "It was him," he said. "God, if Denson's behind this whole thing, I don't know what we're going to do! That guy's a mess!"

"Nicholas, it'll be all right," Elizabeth said soothingly, putting her hand on his arm. She just wished she could convince herself that she really believed that. But she was losing hope.

They had to think of something to save Regina and her parents. But what?

Six

"Have a good day at school, you two!" Mrs. Wakefield called up the stairs.

Elizabeth groaned. "I feel so guilty," she told Jessica, who was fixing her hair at the mirror over Elizabeth's dresser.

"You'd think you were committing some kind of major crime, not just cutting school for a day," Jessica declared. "Besides, today's not going to be fun and games. Going out to Fort Carroll to hunt down this Denson jerk is hardly my idea of a great way to spend a day!"

"I know," Elizabeth said, her expression serious. "Jess, I'm really scared. If this man Denson is as terrible as Nicholas says, won't it be dangerous going out to his house?"

"It could be, but we don't have much choice," Jessica reminded her, giving her hair a furious once-over with the brush. "Denson is the biggest lead we have right now. We can't figure out what Regina heard on the phone. What else are we supposed to do?"

Elizabeth glanced nervously at her watch. "What time did Nicholas say he was picking us up?"

"Nine o'clock," Jessica replied. "Have you got Denson's address?"

Elizabeth nodded. "P. Denson, 1386 Lakewood Drive, Fort Carroll," she read from the piece of paper she'd torn out of her notebook. "That's what the phone book says. He's the only Denson in the area."

"I hope it's the right man." Jessica giggled. "Can you imagine us confronting some poor guy who just happens to be named Denson?"

"Well, it's worth a try." Elizabeth sighed.

An hour later the first part of the mission was completed. Bruce stopped his Porsche across from 1386 Lakewood Drive. It was a small, plain-looking house with a short side driveway leading up to a wooden side door. Nothing special at all, a house like every other one on the block. "That can't be Phillip Denson," Jessica said lightly, pointing at the bare-chested young man mowing the front lawn. He had sandy hair and was good-looking, but didn't look much older than Bruce or Nicholas.

"Does Denson have a son?" Elizabeth asked.

"If that guy is Denson's son, this is our lucky day." Bruce grinned.

"What do you mean?" Nicholas asked, perplexed.

"We just happen," Bruce said mildly, "to have a special weapon with us. Just give Jessica five minutes with that poor sucker, and she'll find out anything we want!"

"Bruce Patman, you shut up!" Jessica said hotly. "Just because you think you—"

"Stop it!" Elizabeth hissed. "Come on, you two, we need to work together, not start arguing with each other. Jess, I think Bruce has a good idea," she added hastily. "He may not have put it very tactfully, but still! What do you think?" she added. "Could you just find out whatever you can from this guy?"

"Oh, all right," Jessica said, mollified. "I'll do what I can."

A minute later Jessica had crossed the small front lawn and stepped right in front of the boy with the mower. He turned the mower off so he could hear her.

Up close the boy was even better-looking than Jessica had first thought, with thick, sandy-blond hair and bright hazel eyes. But something in his expression made him seem aloof.

"Hi," he said, shading his eyes with one hand. "Can I do something for you?" He looked quickly at the Porsche parked across the street and squinted, trying to see the others in the vehicle. "You guys lost or something?"

"No," Jessica said, twirling a lock of blond hair around her finger. "As a matter of fact, we're doing a project for a student newspaper. We're taking a census," she lied.

"A census?" the boy said, looking blank.

Jessica flashed him her most winning smile. "Well, it's actually more like a poll," she amended, lowering her eyes a little. She didn't have to pretend to be interested—the boy really *was* good-looking. "We're looking at different neighborhoods, interviewing homeowners at random," she went on, making her story up as she went along. "We're just asking a few questions. Would you consent to a brief interview? I mean," she added slyly, "you *are* the owner here, aren't you?"

The boy flushed. "My name's Mitch," he said, sticking his hand out awkwardly. "Mitch Denson."

"I'm Jessica," Jessica said sweetly, taking his hand and squeezing it warmly.

Mitch looked nervously around him. "But I'm not the owner," he told her. "My father is."

"What's his name?" Jessica asked, taking out a small notebook and pen from her shoulder bag and trying to look like a real polltaker. "And what sort of work does he do, if you don't mind my asking?"

Mitch looked a little dazed, as if Jessica could

ask him whatever she pleased. "His name is Phillip," he told her. "And he's—well, I guess he calls himself a computer consultant these days."

"Hmmm," Jessica said, writing furiously in her notebook. "That sounds fascinating."

For the next few minutes, Jessica kept asking questions. She asked how many cars the Densons had, whether or not they had a TV, and how often they went out to eat. She was beginning to run out of ideas when to her relief Mitch turned the tables.

He was beginning to relax and enjoy himself a little. "What about you?" he said and grinned. "What do you do with yourself—when you're not driving around asking people questions, that is."

Jessica tossed her hair back and gave Mitch her most alluring smile. "You know," she said softly, running her eyes over his glistening chest and shoulders, "it sure is hot out here today. Do you think there's any chance I could bug you for a glass of something ice-cold?" She looked over his shoulder, toward the house. "If no one's at home . . ." She let her voice trail off suggestively.

Mitch turned bright red. "Uh—as a matter of fact, someone *is* home," he muttered. "My dad said—I mean, my dad's home. He's sleeping." Suddenly Mitch's composure was gone; he seemed nervous.

"Oh." Jessica looked crestfallen."I really *am* thirsty," she reminded him.

"I'll get you a glass of water," Mitch said, hurrying up the front walk to the porch.

"Can't I come in with you?" Jessica asked beseechingly, hurrying after him. "I'll be quiet," she added coyly.

Mitch looked very uncomfortable. "Naw," he said at last. "My father really hates being disturbed. But I'll be back in a minute," he promised. "Don't go away."

"I won't!" Jessica sang out sweetly. The minute the screen door had banged shut behind him, she hurried up the porch steps and leaned over the small railing to look into the living room window.

Jessica wasn't certain exactly what she'd expected to see. But she almost gasped in surprise when she saw Mr. and Mrs. Morrow, right there in the Densons' living room.

Mrs. Morrow jumped to her feet the minute she saw Jessica's face in the window. "Wait!" Jessica mouthed at her, but the next instant Mrs. Morrow was pulling her husband out of sight.

"What are you staring at?" a cross voice beside her demanded.

Jessica whirled around, her heart skipping a beat. Keeping her voice as cool as possible, she reached out for the glass of water Mitch was holding. "Your house is adorable," she cooed. "Just adorable! Sorry to be such a snoop, but I needed to know *exactly* how your living room is furnished. For the poll," she reminded him.

Mitch leaned over the porch rail and peered in the living room window as if to make sure she hadn't seen something she shouldn't have. "Well," he said at last, mollified, "I guess that's all right, if that's all you wanted."

"That's all I wanted," Jessica said perkily, taking several swallows of water and handing him the glass. "Thanks for the drink," she said sweetly. "Now, I'd better be going! We've got two more towns to cover before lunch!"

After flashing Mitch the friendliest smile she could muster, Jessica headed back to the Porsche.

"It was one of the Wakefield twins," Skye Morrow told her husband, pressing her hands to her temples. Mr. and Mrs. Morrow were in the little bedroom that had been designated as theirs since Phillip Denson had brought them to his house. Mrs. Morrow had closed the door tightly behind her, but even so she kept her voice to a whisper. "But I'm not sure which one."

"I wonder what she was doing out here," Mr. Morrow said, shaking his head. "Was she alone?"

"I couldn't tell," his wife whispered back. "All of a sudden I saw her staring into the living room window. That's why I dragged you out of the living room so quickly. I didn't want anyone else to look in and see us."

"I think Phil's still out," Mr. Morrow said, glancing at his watch. "I haven't heard his car in the drive yet."

"If one of the twins knows we're here, they might be able to get in touch with Nicholas," Mrs. Morrow said hopefully. "After all, the twins are friends of Nicholas's, and he might have told them about his trip. . . ." Mrs. Morrow's voice trailed off as she thought about her son. Just then it was hard to imagine she'd ever see him again.

"Look, Skye," her husband said gently, "we've just got to hang on a little bit longer. Denson's bound to crack. Somehow I can't imagine his really carrying out this crazy scheme of his."

Mrs. Morrow hid her face in her hands. She knew her husband too well not to hear the note of fear creeping into his voice. Phillip Denson was a mean little man with grandiose ideas. She wouldn't put anything past him—not anything at all.

From the minute this nightmare had begun, with Denson kidnapping them as they left their house for the airport, Mrs. Morrow's grief and worry had been concentrated on one person: her daughter, Regina. What made her angriest about Denson's plan was that it involved innocent Regina. It made Mrs. Morrow tremble with rage to think of Phillip Denson's girlfriend meeting Regina in Switzerland and hustling her back to Sweet Valley.

Angry as she was, Skye Morrow knew that her best hope of protecting her daughter lay in obedience. Everything Phillip Denson said had to be law as far as she and her husband were concerned. Otherwise, there was no telling what he and his accomplice might do to Regina.

"I'm worried," Mr. Morrow said, looking anxiously out the tiny bedroom window. "If the Wakefield twins are mixed up in this somehow, they could make everything even more complicated than it already is. If Denson catches them snooping around here he could kill us—or them—without giving it a second thought."

Mrs. Morrow looked horrified. She hadn't thought of that. "Or Regina," she whispered. "They could hurt Regina."

Mr. Morrow looked grim. "I just hope they *aren't* involved," he muttered. "Or that if they are, they make damn sure they know what they're doing!"

"You sure took a long time," Bruce drawled as Jessica strolled leisurely back to the car. "What were you doing, writing his biography?"

Jessica frowned. "As a matter of fact, I found out a good deal of valuable information," she retorted. "But if you're going to be such a pain, Bruce, I don't see why I should tell you a thing!"

"For God's sake, you two," Elizabeth cut in, "can't you be sensitive enough to realize that Nicholas doesn't want to put up with your bickering right now?"

Jessica gave Bruce a self-righteous glare before turning to Nicholas. "Don't worry," she assured him. "I saw both your parents. They look perfectly fine. They were right there in the living room!"

Nicholas paled. "My parents. You mean they're in there?" He looked as if he were about to jump out of the car and run inside.

Bruce put his hands firmly on Nicholas's shoulders. "Whoa," he said warningly. "Don't do anything rash. Remember, if we get your parents away from here, Claire Davis is liable to find out before we can get to Regina."

"Sorry." Nicholas buried his head in his hands. "It's so frustrating, knowing they're trapped in there with that—that maniac."

"Well, Mitch isn't a maniac," Jessica said defensively. "In fact, I think he's kind of sweet. He's got really nice shoulders."

"Who cares about his shoulders?" Bruce retorted. "Did you find out anything useful?"

Jessica looked hurt. "I found out he's Phillip Denson's son."

"Uh-oh," Bruce said, turning the key in the ignition. "I think we'd better carry on with this discussion someplace with a little less traffic, folks."

Elizabeth felt her heart skip a beat. The light blue Dodge was pulling up into the short driveway beside the house. "That's the car we saw coming out of the Morrows' driveway!" Elizabeth cried.

Bruce pulled the Porsche away from the curb as the other driver got out of his car.

"That's him all right," Nicholas confirmed grimly. "That's Phillip Denson."

"I can't believe Mitch is really mixed up in all of this," Jessica said mournfully. "He really seemed like a nice guy."

"Nice or not, I'd break his nose right now if I had the chance," Nicholas said harshly.

Elizabeth took a deep breath. Things were getting tenser and tenser as they approached Sweet Valley, and the reason for that was perfectly clear.

Their worst fear had been confirmed. They knew for certain now that Phillip Denson was at the center of everything. The Morrows were as yet unharmed, but who knew how long that would be true?

And what should they do next? Elizabeth wondered. Until they could figure out when Regina was supposed to meet Walter Frank at the plant, they couldn't do much of anything.

Trying to imagine what Regina must be experiencing, Elizabeth felt a lump forming in her throat. Terrible flashbacks of being tied up in Carl's little house kept coming to her as she imagined what Regina might be going through. It made her shudder to remember how frightened and devastatingly alone she'd felt.

Elizabeth was beginning to feel things had gone too far. She didn't care what Regina's note had said. She wished they had gone to the police after all.

Seven

"Look, Liz," Jessica said, picking up a slip of paper from the kitchen counter. "Mom must've come home from work earlier this afternoon. She left a message for you."

Elizabeth hurried over to read the note. "Liz—someone named Suzanne called at three o'clock from the office at school. She asked you to call her back when you get a chance."

Jessica laughed. "Boy, Liz, from the expression on your face, you'd think you'd just gotten arrested."

Elizabeth sighed. "I'm not used to cutting school," she replied. "I hope this message is completely unrelated."

Biting her lip, Elizabeth dialed the number of the main office at Sweet Valley High. It was four o'clock already, and on a Friday afternoon she half expected the office to be closed. But on the third ring someone picked up the phone.

"I'm calling to speak to Suzanne," Elizabeth said. "Is she there, please?"

"This is Suzanne," a young-sounding voice responded. "Who's this?"

"Elizabeth Wakefield. I just got home and found a message here that you'd called."

"Liz!" The girl sounded pleased. "This is Suzanne Hanlon."

"Oh, hi, Suzanne," Elizabeth said pleasantly. Suzanne was a tall, willowy sophomore with silky, dark hair and wide-set hazel eyes. She wasn't someone Elizabeth knew very well. She did know, mostly from Jessica, that Suzanne's family was extremely well off. Privately, Elizabeth thought Suzanne was a little bit affected. She seemed to like giving everyone at school the impression that she was sophisticated and very cultured. But Elizabeth didn't want to judge her.

"What can I do for you, Suzanne?" she asked.

"Well, I wanted to talk to you about the literary evening the Honor Society is putting on in two weeks," Suzanne said. "Sorry to be calling you from the office, but I've been doing some special work for the principal, and I'm here all the time these days!"

Elizabeth was thoughtful. School seemed so far away at the moment. Regina and her parents were uppermost in her mind. Still, she felt bad again about having missed her classes.

"Tell me about the evening," Elizabeth said. "What are you planning?"

"Well, that's what I wanted to talk to you about," Suzanne said. "I wondered if one or two of you from *The Oracle* might want to get involved. That is, if you've got the time," she added pointedly.

"Well, what did you have in mind?" Elizabeth asked again.

"Oh, you know," Suzanne said airily. "Something simple, like readings. I thought we'd have a few student poets read, a few short-story writers, and maybe—"

"Who's working on the reading with you?"

"Well, no one, really," Suzanne admitted.

Elizabeth sighed. It sounded to her as though Suzanne's plans were a little sophisticated for Sweet Valley High. But perhaps she had something she'd written that was suitable. "I don't know about anyone else on the *Oracle* staff," Elizabeth said, "but I'd be happy to read something. Just let me know when and where, and I'll be there."

"What was that all about?" Jessica demanded a moment later, after Elizabeth had hung up the receiver. "Did the office catch up with the year's most dangerous truant, or are they going to let you off the hook this time?"

"Very funny," Elizabeth retorted. "As a matter of fact, it wasn't really the office that wanted me at all," she admitted. "It was Suzanne Hanlon."

Jessica groaned and held her sides. "Ugh! Old Hands-Off Hanlon! What did *she* want?"

"Jessica!" Elizabeth exclaimed, laughing. "*What* did you call her?"

Jessica giggled. "That's what the guys call her," she explained. "She's a real pain. She's always trying to run the show at the sorority—but you wouldn't know, since you never come to any of our meetings!"

The twins were both members of Pi Beta Alpha, a very exclusive sorority at school. But Elizabeth had only joined at Jessica's insistence. She found the sorority cliquish and boring, whereas Jessica thought it was simply wonderful.

"Why is she such a pain?" Elizabeth asked, opening the refrigerator and taking out a carton of milk.

Jessica wrinkled her nose. "I don't know," she said, thinking it over. "She's just kind of—well, not really stuck-up. But she always acts like she knows what's right. You know what I mean? Sort of a know-it-all. Her parents are loaded, though," she concluded.

Elizabeth frowned. "I'm just trying to figure out . . . oh, never mind," she laughed. "Something tells me I'll find out more than I want to about Suzanne. She's organizing a literary evening for the Honor Society, and it sounds as if she wants some help, as well as some readers!"

"I'd be willing to read the hottest parts of my diary," Jessica suggested. "That would draw crowds!"

Elizabeth groaned. "I'm not sure that's very literary," she retorted, pouring herself a glass of juice.

Despite her teasing tone, Elizabeth really was curious about Suzanne Hanlon. The girl had struck her as being standoffish, even aloof. Maybe the reading would provide a chance to get to know her better.

But Elizabeth's mind was busy with much more serious matters. She and Jessica were supposed to meet Nicholas and Bruce at the Patmans' the next day. Between now and then, Elizabeth wanted to devise some kind of plan to save Regina and her parents.

"Where are you going?" Jessica demanded as Elizabeth headed out the kitchen, holding the glass of juice.

"Outside!" Elizabeth called over her shoulder, struggling with the sliding door leading out to the patio. She had a lot of brainstorming to do. And she thought she'd be able to do her best thinking alone.

Regina opened her eyes with a start. "I must've been dreaming," she said aloud, running her hand over her face and sitting up in the darkened room. It was so hard to tell anymore what time it was! She had accidentally unplugged the alarm clock on her night table and hadn't bothered to reset it.

It just didn't seem to matter what time it was anymore. Regina's eyes filled with tears. It felt like ages since the day she had received the note from Bruce and the twins. She'd been certain that they could help somehow, but she had heard nothing since then. Now Regina was beginning to feel desperate.

The previous night Claire's partner, who Regina had heard Claire call Phil, had come over again, and he and Claire had locked themselves in Regina's father's study, talking in low voices. Regina was afraid to stand outside the door and try to listen. It was incredibly frustrating, knowing that just down the stairs they were making plans so vital to her well-being.

At last Phil had come upstairs. "We want to make sure you know exactly what you're supposed to do," he said roughly. "I'm not going to mince my words," he added. " A lot's riding on you. If you make any mistakes, or if you try anything funny—well, we both just want you to understand that we've warned you."

Regina stared dully at the floor. *Just shoot me now,* she wanted to tell him. *Just end this agony right here and now!*

Phil's expression suddenly turned ugly. "Just

don't make a mistake," he repeated. "Remember, you've got to think about your parents, too."

With that, he'd pulled her door shut, leaving her alone again.

Regina trembled violently every time she remembered that scene. It was bad enough being locked up with Claire, living in fear all the time. But hearing Phil threaten to hurt her parents. . . . That horrified Regina.

Regina adored both her parents, but she'd always felt a special gratitude and admiration for her mother. Although Mrs. Morrow had tried to keep it from her, Regina knew her handicap had caused her mother to feel endless guilt and unhappiness. Her mother had been taking medication while she was pregnant and blamed herself for Regina's deafness. For years Mrs. Morrow had suffered from blinding headaches. The doctors couldn't find a cause, but Regina and Nicholas knew what brought them on. Whenever she felt guilty over Regina's deafness, Mrs. Morrow's headaches came back.

Finally, after all these years, her parents' patient letters of inquiry to doctors all over the world had met with a positive response. Dr. Friederich, a world-renowned surgeon in Switzerland, had invented a series of special treatments that he felt confident would work on Regina.

After a good deal of heartache and conflict,

Regina had decided to leave Sweet Valley to have the treatments. It had been hard to leave her family, and even harder to leave her new friends. But she knew in the long run it would be worth it.

And the treatments had worked! Her hearing wasn't perfect yet, but it was much, much better.

For months, while she was in Switzerland, Regina had dreamed about her homecoming. She'd imagined running up to Bruce and throwing her arms around his neck and actually being able to hear the magical words "I love you" from his lips. She and Bruce had separated on bad terms. An angry misunderstanding had preceded her decision to go to Bern, and though they had long since made up in loving letters, they hadn't had the opportunity to forgive each other in person. Regina had dreamed so often of that moment, and she'd dreamed of having a huge party in the Morrow mansion, opening up the estate to all her friends from Sweet Valley High. Most of all, she'd dreamed of taking her mother's hands, looking straight into her eyes, and telling her how much she loved her and how grateful she was for everything her mother had done.

Looking around her dark bedroom, Regina laughed bitterly. "I guess this isn't exactly the kind of reception I had in mind." She groaned, and swung her legs over the side of her bed.

The very worst thing was how hopeless she

felt. More than once, she had seriously considered trying to escape from the house. She could have negotiated the half-mile to Bruce's place with a blindfold on, she knew the neighborhood so well. She'd planned her escape over and over again, down to the last detail.

But even as she planned, she knew it was hopeless. Suppose she managed to make it to Bruce's house before Claire woke up? Then what? She could call the police and hope against hope that they could find her parents before Claire discovered she was gone. But who knew where her parents were? It wouldn't take long for Claire to find out that she was missing. One phone call and Denson would carry out his terrible threats. Her mother . . .

Regina shook her head, tears welling up in her eyes. That was a chance she'd never take.

Escape was out of the question. All Regina could do was sit there, waiting for Denson and Claire to use her as a pawn in their crime.

Sit there and pray, Regina thought miserably. It was beginning to look as if there was nothing Bruce or the twins could do to save her and her parents!

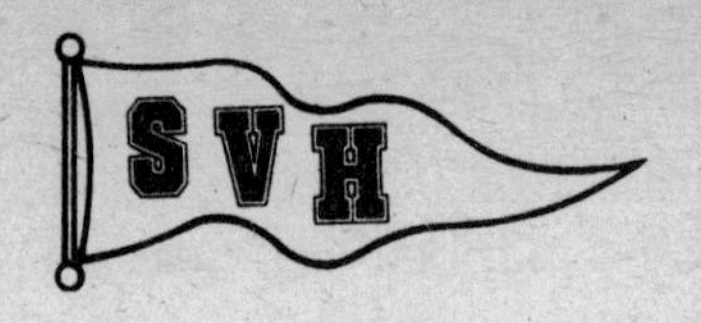

Eight

"Can I get anyone anything else to drink? Coffee or tea?" Bruce asked, coming out to the patio with a tray of sandwiches and a large pitcher of juice. It was early Saturday afternoon.

Jessica shook her head, marveling. "Your parents should go away more often, Bruce. You're turning into an independent bachelor right before our eyes!"

Bruce looked sheepish. "Actually, Maria left the sandwiches out," he admitted. Maria was the Patmans' cook. Everyone laughed, and the tension that had settled over the four eased somewhat.

"OK," Bruce said, setting the tray and the pitcher on the table, then sitting down. "First things first. We've got to come up with the very best plan for a simultaneous rescue. But to do that, we need to figure out when Denson's planning on stealing the prototype chip. Liz, have you got Regina's note?"

Elizabeth nodded and passed him the piece of paper. It had been read and reread so many times by now that it was practically falling to pieces.

"Read the paragraph again about overhearing Claire talking about taking Regina to the plant," Nicholas suggested. "The part where she says the 'money is heaven' stuff."

"OK," Elizabeth said. "Now, listen really carefully, you guys. If we could figure out what she means by this, I think we'd have it cracked." Taking a deep breath, Elizabeth read the paragraph aloud.

> "Claire and her friend are planning on using me to steal the microchip from my father's plant. They've told me everything but when. I keep trying to find out, but I'm not getting anywhere. I tried to figure out what Claire said last night on the phone. It sounded like 'money is heaven.' That was all I could make out."

"Money is heaven," Bruce said dully. "That puts us right back to square one. What on earth is that supposed to mean?"

They were all quiet for a minute, turning the three words over and over again in their minds.

"Forget the code," Bruce said at last. "Let's try

to be logical about this. Today is Saturday. The plant's closed, right?"

"Right," Nicholas confirmed. "It's closed all weekend."

"Well, if you were Phillip Denson, how do you think you'd be feeling right now? The guy's got one of the richest men in the Valley locked up in his living room along with his wife. Worse, he's got their only daughter being held hostage up at the estate. The point is, he's taking some risks. The Morrows are pretty high-profile in this town, and it's not going to take much longer before somebody misses them—somebody besides us."

"Bruce has a point," Elizabeth chimed in. "If Denson's smart, he'll want to get this thing over with fast. The longer he drags it out, the greater his chances of being nailed."

Nicholas looked thoughtful. "I'd agree with you," he said at last, "except how do we know that someone as slimy as Denson uses the same kind of logic we do? This guy may be sick, remember? How do we know what he's planning?"

"Nicholas," Bruce said quietly, "we've got to do something. And all we can do is think rationally. Phil Denson may be sick, but that doesn't mean he isn't capable of logic. How late does the plant stay open during the week?"

Nicholas thought a moment. "Most of the employees leave at five, but the place doesn't officially close until six. And Walter, the manager, doesn't lock up until a little bit later."

"OK," Bruce said, picking up a pad of paper from the patio table and jotting something down with a freshly sharpened pencil. "Let's assume that Denson wants to move fast. That he plans to take Regina over to the plant on Monday—but after everyone's gone. Everyone but Walter, that is."

"Hey!" Jessica shrieked, bouncing up from her chair. "I've got it! I've broken the code!"

Everyone stared blankly at her. "What are you talking about?" Elizabeth demanded.

Jessica's eyes were shining. "I mean it," she insisted. "Put your hands over your ears, all three of you. Tell me what it sounds like I'm saying. Think of a day and a time."

Elizabeth, Bruce, and Nicholas looked at each other and shrugged. But Jessica was too excited to ignore. Putting their hands over their ears, they listened to the slightly muffled sound as Jessica repeated over and over again, "Money is heaven. Money is heaven. Money is—"

"Monday at seven!" Elizabeth cried, jumping to her feet and throwing her arms around her twin. "Jess, you've done it! You've broken the code!"

"It was nothing," Jessica said modestly, sitting down again and looking triumphantly at Bruce. "I told you reading all those mysteries would pay off one day, Liz."

"Good work," Bruce said grudgingly. "I've got to hand it to you, Jessica. You're a pretty good detective."

"Money is heaven," Nicholas repeated wonderingly. "So Regina overheard Claire saying 'Monday at seven.' It seems like our best lead."

"We'll have to assume that's what it means," Bruce agreed. "It's not just our best lead, it's our *only* lead!"

"Monday at seven it is, then," Jessica said. "Now that we know *when*, we've got to come up with a way to rescue Regina and Mr. and Mrs. Morrow at the same time."

Everyone was quiet again. At last, Elizabeth spoke up. "I think I've come up with a plan," she said shyly. "I'm not sure it'll work," she added hastily, "and it's got one giant drawback. But it's the best I can do."

"Let's hear it!" Nicholas cried.

"Well," Elizabeth began, "our problem has been finding a time when we could free your parents without endangering Regina, or vice versa. Right?"

Nicholas nodded.

"Well, what if we could release your parents while Regina's in the plant with Claire? That's the one time we know for sure Regina will be safe. Claire won't be able to find out we've freed the Morrows—and she wouldn't be able to do anything to Regina, even if she *did* find out. The plant is guarded, right?"

"Yes," Nicholas assured her. "No one can get in without first being cleared by the security guard."

"And Claire has to act like she's Regina's aunt, or her cover's blown!" Elizabeth went on. "Here's what we do," she continued, gaining confidence as she went on. "Nicholas and I will go to the plant. Jessica, you and Bruce will go out to Fort Carroll. At exactly seven o'clock, you two will break into Phillip Denson's house and release the Morrows. Meanwhile, Nicholas and I will be at the plant, waiting for Regina and Claire to come out. When they do, I'll intercept Claire and Regina. I don't know how I can stall them, but I'll think of something. And while I'm stalling them, Nicholas can call the police."

Jessica wrinkled her nose. "It sounds awfully complicated," she objected. "I can already think of a million things that could go wrong. How are you going to stall Regina and this Claire woman, for one thing?"

Elizabeth looked worried. "I don't know," she admitted. "Any ideas?"

Jessica giggled. "You could always trip her," she suggested.

"I don't think Liz's plan is a bad one," Nicholas said slowly, thinking it over. "It *is* complicated, but I don't think there's any way we can carry this off with a simple plan. My question is this," he added. "Where's Denson supposed to be during this whole thing? Have we got any idea at all?"

Bruce whistled under his breath. "We don't know, do we?" he said. "Do you suppose he's planning to meet Claire and Regina at the plant?"

"God knows what he's planning." Nicholas sighed. "At this point, I wouldn't put anything past him."

Jessica looked nervous. "You know, I don't like the sound of this. Isn't there some way we could arrange for the police to be there beforehand?"

Bruce shook his head. "We can't risk that, Jess. What if they insist on going straight over to the Morrows' place? That would put Regina in a hell of a spot!"

"Well, I think we should go with Liz's plan," Nicholas repeated. "But we've got to figure out some way to find out where Phillip Denson's going to be Monday night."

Everyone was quiet again for a minute.

"Jessica—" Bruce began imploringly.

Jessica blinked. "What?" she demanded as Nicholas and Elizabeth turned to look at her, too. "What is it? Why are you all staring at me?"

"You did such a good job talking to Mitch yesterday," Nicholas reminded her. "If it weren't for you, we wouldn't know *half* as much as we know now."

"No way," Jessica said stubbornly. "I'm

beginning to think I don't like being a detective one bit!"

"Come on, Jess," Elizabeth begged her. "Just one more time! You're the only one who can help us find out where Denson's going to be!"

Jessica bit her lower lip. "Oh, all right," she said at last, not looking very happy about the latest turn in the conversation. "I'll try. But I can't promise anything," she reminded them quickly.

"I wouldn't worry about that." Bruce laughed. "With Jessica as bait, I have a feeling Mitch will swallow it all, hook, line, and sinker!"

"Speaking of sinking," Jessica said, jumping up from the table and pinning Bruce's arms back so he couldn't move, "how would you feel about a little swim, Mr. Patman? I have a feeling it would really help cool you off!"

Elizabeth couldn't help laughing as she watched her sister trying to throw Bruce in the pool. Suddenly she felt a million times better. They actually had a plan—and a strong lead on when the microchip prototype was supposed to be stolen.

It was a beginning. And if Jessica could find out from Mitch where Phillip Denson was going to be, they just might be able to pull this thing off.

They *would* pull this thing off, Elizabeth corrected herself. There couldn't be a single element of doubt in anyone's mind. They simply had too much at stake to lose confidence in themselves now!

After a great deal of discussion, the four decided there wasn't much more they could do that afternoon. "I think we should go to the beach," Jessica announced.

Nicholas didn't look happy about Jessica's suggestion.

"There's nothing we can do now," Jessica reminded him. "I promise, I'll go over to the Densons' tomorrow and try to find Mitch. But today's practically shot anyway!"

Elizabeth agreed. "We need to take our minds off everything, if we possibly can," she said gently, smiling at Nicholas. "And we need to keep calm so we'll be ready on Monday night. Maybe a little sand and sun wouldn't be such a bad idea!"

In the end it was Bruce who convinced Nicholas. "Look, I understand how you feel," he said in a low voice. "You know how much I love Regina. It makes me sick thinking about her, trapped, less than a mile from here! There's nothing worse than feeling helpless. But we can't do anything right now. Besides," he concluded, ending the argument, "you're my houseguest this week. And I say a trip to the beach would do us good, so that's that!"

An hour or so later, the four were spread out

on towels on the warm white sand, watching the sparkling waves of the Pacific. "You were right, Jess," Elizabeth whispered. "Look at him. He's out like a light!"

Nicholas hadn't been able to sleep since Bruce had called him in San Francisco. And no sooner had he stretched out on his towel than he'd fallen fast asleep.

"I don't blame him." Bruce sighed and stretched out. "I'm pretty tired myself. I guess we all are! I've been so worried about Regina. Plus all this centennial stuff is really piling up—as if I could concentrate on it now!"

"Why? What's the problem?" Jessica asked.

Bruce sighed. "Well, the first thing is that I need someone to organize a big community picnic. It's a really important part of the centennial, and I just can't plan it along with everything else." He looked imploringly at Jessica. "In fact, Jess, I sort of wondered if you—"

"You want *me* to run the picnic?" Jessica demanded, her aqua eyes widening.

"It would be such a big help if you could, Jess," Bruce said.

Jessica had a feeling for once that Bruce was really being sincere. "OK," she said impulsively. "I'll do it. Does that solve your problem?"

"Part of it. But I'm still worried about Ken Matthews."

"I've been meaning to ask you about that, Bruce," Jessica said. "About the big football game coming up against Palisades—I heard a rumor that Ken Matthews may not be playing. Lila Fowler said he's doing so badly in English that he's probably going to get kicked off the team!"

"Yeah," Bruce grumbled. "I don't know what his problem is. Junior English is really easy!"

"Right, Bruce," Jessica said sarcastically. She thought Bruce occasionally acted as if he were ten years older than she and her sister, instead of just one and a half!

"Bruce is right, though," Elizabeth pointed out, keeping her voice down so as not to wake Nicholas. "It may not exactly be easy, but it's not difficult! And Ken's never had any problems before."

"It's easy for you," Jessica pointed out. "But you want to be a writer, remember? For the rest of us, it isn't half as easy."

Elizabeth looked thoughtful. "Poor Ken. He's been looking forward to the centennial game for ages!"

"Yeah," Bruce said. "So have we all! Only without Ken playing, Palisades is going to stomp all over us!"

Elizabeth frowned. "You really think we'd lose without Ken?"

Bruce crossed his arms behind his neck. "I'm sure of it. Palisades has got an amazing quarterback, a guy named Peter Straus. He's already being recruited by all the big colleges. And without Ken to match him, we're shot!"

Elizabeth was thoughtful for a minute. "Well, maybe he'll be able to pull his grade up. The game's still a few weeks off."

Jessica rolled over on her stomach. "Maybe *you* can help Ken pull his grade up," she suggested sleepily. "You're the ace writer, Liz."

Elizabeth was quiet for a minute. Maybe she *should* offer to help Ken. It wouldn't be hard. She could just give him a couple of pointers on his papers. Actually, it might be kind of fun.

Elizabeth closed her eyes too. Like the others, she was incredibly tired, and the combination of sun and sea air was so soothing she was getting drowsy. Before she drifted off, she made a mental note to approach Ken about his English grade—after Monday night, when the Morrows were safe and sound and the four teenage detectives could go back to leading normal lives again!

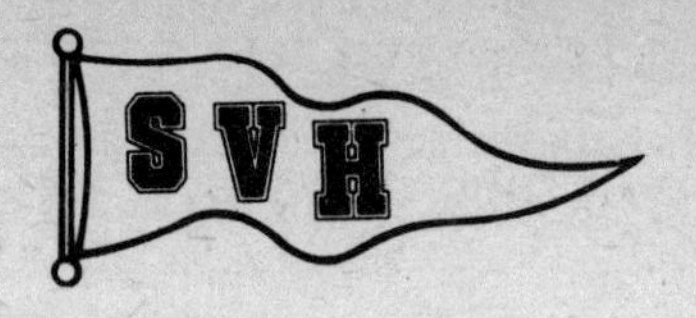

Nine

It was Sunday morning, and Skye Morrow felt as if she and her husband had been trapped in Phillip Denson's house for a millennium. As long as she lived, she would never forget the day Denson had stopped their car as they pulled out onto the road from their driveway, surprising the two of them as they were leaving for the airport.

"What are we going to do?" Skye Morrow asked her husband for what must have been the dozenth time. Mr. Morrow didn't answer. He was beginning to lose hope, too, Mrs. Morrow realized with alarm. He wasn't even trying to reassure her anymore!

Mrs. Morrow and her husband were sitting alone at the small table in the Densons' cramped kitchen. Mitch had made them breakfast, but neither of them had any appetite.

"That sounds like my dad," Mitch said

nervously, sticking his head into the kitchen. "I just thought I'd let you two know he's come back."

Mrs. Morrow shook her head. "He's the same age as Nicholas," she said sadly after Mitch had walked away. "I really feel sorry for him. With Phil Denson for a father, what kind of chance does he have to lead a normal life?"

Mr. Morrow shrugged. "Right now I'm not so sure Regina is very lucky, either," he said moodily. "God, Skye, I want to kill myself every time I think what she must be going through back at the house! If this is what running a successful business means, exposing my daughter to this kind of danger—"

Mrs. Morrow put her hand over his on the table. "It wasn't your fault!" she interrupted. "Honey, you've taken every precaution—you always have! In all the years I've known you, you've never done a dishonest thing. What else could anyone expect of a man?"

Mr. Morrow shook his head. "My business is very high-profile. I get so much publicity. I feel . . . I don't know. I keep wondering. Maybe if I hadn't tried to develop this new chip, maybe Phil wouldn't have gotten this crazy revenge scheme in his head."

"That's nonsense," Mrs. Morrow said loyally. "You're a hard-working businessman and a loving and devoted father. You've worked for years to develop this chip, and you weren't doing it for power or money! You have a keen mind, and you wanted to satisfy yourself, to see if you could meet the challenge."

Mr. Morrow sighed and hung his head. "I feel so terrible about you and Regina," he said finally. "Darling, I could stand this if the danger were just directed at me! But to think of you or Regina getting hurt just tears me up inside."

Mrs. Morrow squeezed his hand as hard as she could. "I love you," she said softly, looking deep into his eyes. "Kurt, I truly believe we're going to be all right. I don't know why, but suddenly I feel hopeful again."

"Well, keep your spirits up," Mr. Morrow said, squeezing her hand.

Just then the kitchen door swung open, and Phillip Denson came in, a toothpick dangling from his mouth. Mrs. Morrow felt terrible again the minute she saw him.

"Hope I'm not interrupting anything here," he drawled, leaning back against the counter. "Just thought I'd come in and see how you folks are doing this morning. Hope you got a good night's sleep," he added languidly, taking the toothpick out and looking at it for a minute before throwing it into the trash can. " 'Cause you're sure going to need to be rested up. We've got ourselves a busy week ahead."

Mr. Morrow gave his wife a warning look. *Don't let him scare you,* it said. But Mrs. Morrow looked scared anyway.

"What's the plan, Phil?" Mr. Morrow asked. "Or don't you feel like letting us in on any of the specifics yet?"

Phillip Denson laughed nastily. "You might as well know," he answered, crossing his arms and looking smug. "It can't make much difference at this point."

"Go on," Mr. Morrow said grimly. "Why don't you fill us in?"

"Well, tomorrow morning you're going to call Walter Frank at the plant and tell him your trip to Europe is taking longer than you planned. And you've found out that you need the microchip prototype you've got locked up in the safe in the plant, only you don't have time to come get it yourself. So you're sending Regina over to get it with her aunt Claire." Suddenly Phillip Denson looked really mean. "Did you follow that?"

Mr. Morrow took a deep breath. After a minute he nodded.

"Good," Denson snapped. "Make sure you don't forget it. Then you'll tell Frank that Regina and her aunt will be at the plant at seven o'clock. Tell him to have the chip and the plans ready and waiting. We're going to be in a hurry by then."

"So what next?" Mr. Morrow asked roughly. "What are you going to do once you've got the chip, Phil?"

"Sell it." Phillip Denson laughed and snapped

his fingers. "There's a man down in Rio de Janeiro who's pretty eager to buy that little chip of yours. And he's going to give me a pretty penny for it, too. Once I've made the sale, I'm going to be one rich man." Denson gave a grin that made Mrs. Morrow's flesh crawl. "One rich man," he repeated, smiling horribly.

"What about us?" Mrs. Morrow asked weakly, her eyes filling with tears. "Once you've got the plans and the chip, what are you going to do with us?"

The kitchen was terribly quiet for a minute. "I wouldn't lose any sleep worrying about that," Denson said finally. "You just do what you're told, and we'll see what kind of bargain we can make."

With that, he stormed out of the kitchen, leaving the Morrows alone again.

Mrs. Morrow felt she couldn't look her husband in the eyes. Phillip Denson couldn't possibly let them go, she was thinking. Someone as cunning as Denson wouldn't leave his tracks uncovered that way! He'd be afraid the Morrows would go straight to the police.

Suddenly Mrs. Morrow realized why her husband had been acting so listless, so peculiar. He had realized this long ago. He had known for days that it wasn't just the microchip or the fate of his computer business they were fighting for. They were fighting for their lives—all three of them. And it was beginning to look as though they were going to lose the battle.

Jessica frowned as she looked around her. It was Sunday morning, and Lakewood Drive was almost completely deserted, except for a little girl playing hopscotch on the sidewalk.

Screwing up her courage, Jessica walked up the narrow flagstone path to the front porch of number 1386. "I hope Mitch is home," she murmured as she walked up the steps. The thought of running into Phillip Denson by herself wasn't very appealing.

Jessica had thought carefully about what to wear and had decided on a blue denim miniskirt and a halter top. From the brief impression she'd gotten of Mitch Denson, those seemed like the sort of clothes he'd like best on a girl. And pleasing Mitch was what Jessica intended to do that day.

She pushed the door bell and nervously brushed her hair back with one hand. It was a full minute before anyone came to the door. Jessica thought she noticed a curtain rustling, and wondered if someone was looking outside to see who it was before opening the door. At last the front door opened, and Mitch stuck his head outside.

"Jessica!" he cried, his face lighting up.

Jessica lowered her eyes, trying to look shy

and charming at the same time. It wasn't easy, but Mitch didn't seem to care.

"You can't come in!" he added in a hoarse whisper. Realizing how abrupt he sounded, his face reddened. "Uh, I mean my dad's sleeping again," he muttered, sidling outside onto the porch and shutting the door firmly behind him. He was wearing track shorts and a cut-off T-shirt. Jessica thought he looked terrific, though his small talk needed a little bit of refining.

"Boy," Jessica said, smiling at him, "your father sure does sleep a lot. Anyway, the reason I came over is I wanted to invite you to come to a beach party with me. It's going to be lots of fun," she added, fixing her blue-green eyes beseechingly on his face. "I'd really love it if you'd be my date, Mitch."

"I'd like to," Mitch said, his eyes lighting up. "That would be really nice, Jessica. But I'm kind of—well, I'm doing a lot of stuff for my dad around the house lately. I'm really tied up."

"You didn't even ask when the beach party is," Jessica reproached him, pouting. "I guess you just don't like me very much, huh?"

Mitch turned red. "No! I mean, yes, Jessica. I like you a lot! I'd love to go with you," he added miserably. "When is the party?"

"Monday night," Jessica told him. "It's nothing formal, just volleyball and dancing up at Castle Cove. You can come just as you are right now," she added, running her eyes appreciatively up his narrow torso to his broad shoulders.

"Monday night, huh?" Mitch frowned. "That's kind of a bad night for me, as a matter of fact."

Jessica put on her best hurt look. "Oh," she said in a small voice. "You've already got a date?"

"Well, sort of." Mitch didn't say anything else, and Jessica could tell there wasn't much more she could get out of him just then.

"Is your dad going to be taking a nap on Monday night?" she asked, trying to sound seductive. "If he isn't, maybe I could come by here instead of going to the beach. Would you like that?"

Mitch grew even redder. "Yeah," he said. "That'd be great, Jessica. Only I'm not sure—"

He looked furtively behind him, and Jessica could tell he was going to make an excuse any second to go back inside. "Why don't I just come by on Monday night, then?" she purred. "That way we can see how busy you are." She dropped her voice and reached out to run her hand along Mitch's strong forearm. "How would that be?" she asked.

Mitch gulped. "That sounds great," he said finally. "But I'm not sure if I—"

"Don't worry about a thing," Jessica interrupted hastily. "I'll just swing by around seven or so. If you're busy, I'll go on to the party alone. OK?"

"OK," Mitch said weakly, staring at her as if under a spell.

Whew, Jessica thought, hurrying back down the front walk to the red Fiat Spider. She'd been afraid for a minute that Mitch wasn't going to let her make a date.

In fact, things hadn't gone quite the way Jessica had planned. She had hoped Mitch would open up a little, maybe invite her over on Monday night. That way she could have found out for sure whether or not his father was going to be home. But getting information out of Mitch was proving to be a lot harder than she'd expected. The minute Jessica mentioned his father, Mitch looked so nervous she was afraid he was going to faint.

She had done the very best she could, she told herself, turning the key in the ignition and starting up the Fiat. It wasn't her fault Mitch was so incredibly flustered all the time. Anyway, she thought, she would have both good news and bad news to report to her three detective partners when she got back to Sweet Valley.

The good news was that she and Mitch had a date for Monday night at seven. Maybe not exactly a date, but he was certainly expecting her.

The bad news was that she still had no idea

where Phillip Denson was going to be Monday evening. And Jessica had a feeling that in this instance, the bad news was going to figure more prominently than the good when she recounted the events of her journey to Bruce, Nicholas, and Elizabeth later that afternoon!

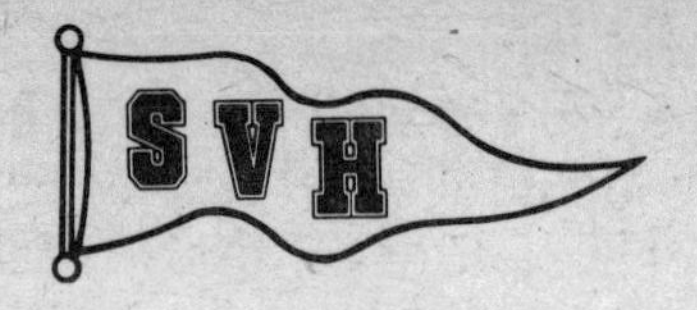

Ten

When Mr. Morrow woke up Monday morning, Phillip Denson was standing next to the bed, pointing a revolver directly at him. "Get out of bed," Denson said evenly, "and do exactly what I tell you. Things are starting to happen," he added, smiling strangely at his former employer. "It's Monday. Things are starting to happen!"

Mr. Morrow felt a cold sweat breaking out on his brow. He kept his gaze fixed on the barrel of Denson's gun as he climbed slowly out of bed.

"Hurry up!" Phillip Denson barked, gesturing toward the door with the gun. "We've got a call to make, Kurt."

Mrs. Morrow had woken up now, too. Her husband could feel her trembling next to him. "I'll be all right," he whispered, squeezing her hand. Phillip Denson glared at him, and he walked evenly through the door, keeping his head high. Denson followed him, pressing the gun against his ribs.

"Now, get on the phone," Denson ordered him roughly, pointing at the telephone on the living room table. "And get Walter Frank on the line. Remember what I told you to say yesterday?"

Mr. Morrow ran his hand over his unshaven chin. "Yes," he said, trying to clear his head. "I think so. Regina's coming to pick up the chip prototype and the plans for the new generation MicroTech. She'll be at the plant at seven o'clock tonight. Is that right?"

"You got it. And make sure you tell him to be on time. Tell him Regina's got a plane to a catch."

Mr. Morrow sighed. Picking up the receiver, he dialed the number of the plant. It felt as though it were barely dawn, but according to the clock on the living room wall, it was 9:05.

"Walter? It's Kurt," he said, trying hard to keep his voice even. Phillip Denson cocked the revolver at him, aiming it directly at his chest. Mr. Morrow took a deep breath.

"Mr. Morrow? I thought you were in Switzerland!" Walter Frank said, sounding confused. "When did you get back?"

"I'm still here," Mr. Morrow said heavily, staring dully at Denson's gun. "In Bern. Things are taking a little longer over here than I'd expected."

Walter was quiet for a minute. "You're calling from Europe?" he said. "It sounds like you're just in the next town!"

"Yeah, well, these connections get better all the time," Mr. Morrow said, frowning at Denson. "Look, Walter, I can't stay on the phone. I have a very important favor to ask of you. I'm meeting with some people the day after tomorrow who want to see the plans for the MicroTech. They want to see it all—the plans and the chip prototype. I don't want to use a courier service—the chip is too valuable. So I'm sending my daughter over to the plant to pick it up from you tonight. Can you have it ready for her? She'll be in a hurry; she's got to catch a plane back to Bern tonight."

Walter Frank was quiet for a minute. "Excuse me, sir, but are you sure? I mean, the chip is—"

"Walter," Mr. Morrow said firmly, "have it ready for her, please. She'll be coming to the front entrance of the plant at seven o'clock. Can you hear me?"

"Yes, sir," Walter Frank said weakly. "Sorry for asking, sir, but I just thought—"

"Hang up," Denson whispered suddenly, gesturing at Mr. Morrow with the gun. "I mean it. Hang up."

"Goodbye, Walter," Mr. Morrow said. Without another word, he placed the receiver on the hook.

"Fine," Phillip Denson said. "That was fine. You think he got it all?" he asked uncertainly.

"I should think so," Mr. Morrow replied. "Walter's not stupid, Phil. He should be able to follow the instructions I just gave him."

"Let's hope so—for your sake. Because if anything goes wrong, Kurt, and I mean *anything*, that little wife of yours in there is going to get it. You understand?"

Mr. Morrow didn't answer. Seven o'clock, he thought grimly, looking again at the clock on the wall. He suspected that this was going to be one of the longest days in his entire life.

"I can't ever remember being so scared," Jessica whispered to Elizabeth. It was five-thirty, and the twins were sitting by the Patmans' pool, waiting for Nicholas and Bruce so they could run over last-minute instructions before splitting up.

"God, I just hope everything goes all right," Elizabeth whispered. "Feel my hand," she added. "It's like ice!"

"Are you two ready?" Bruce called, crossing over to join them on the lawn. "Nicholas said he'd be out in a minute. Poor guy," he added sympathetically. "He's a complete wreck. He's so afraid something might go wrong tonight!"

"I was just telling Jessica that we should run over the plans again, just to make sure," Elizabeth said.

Bruce nodded. "Here comes Nicholas," he said at last. "OK. Should we run over it again, from the top?"

Nicholas sat down beside the twins. "Go on," he said, his voice breaking a little.

"Nicholas, you and Liz will head over to the plant in the Fiat," Bruce said, consulting his note pad. "Since the Jeep has a phone in it, Jessica and I will drive it. Now, Nicholas, you say there's a pay phone just out of sight of the main entrance of the plant, right?"

Nicholas nodded.

"Well, that's your post," Bruce said. "Remember, you have two calls to make. Do you have enough change?"

Nicholas laughed uneasily. "Yes," he answered, checking the pocket of his jeans just to make sure.

"Now, you make the first call to Jessica and me. Call the minute you see Regina entering the plant with Claire. Remember, call as soon as she enters—not when she comes out. OK?"

Nicholas nodded.

"That'll be the signal to Jessica and me. It'll mean that Regina's safe in the plant, and we'll ambush the Denson house, get the Morrows, and drive over to the plant as fast as we can. Your second call," he continued, "is to the police. And you make that—"

"While I'm stalling Claire and Regina," Elizabeth interrupted.

"Right!" Bruce snapped his fingers. "We've really got this down." He grinned. "We're going to be famous after tonight!"

Nobody responded to that. Elizabeth hoped that they'd be able to pull this thing off. The timing was critical—dangerously so. But this plan was their only hope!

Suddenly Bruce looked scared, too. "I'll tell you what," he suggested. "Let's make that three phone calls, Nicholas. Why don't you call me as soon as you and Liz have assumed your positions in front of the plant, OK?"

"OK," Nicholas said heavily, picking up his jacket and handing the Jeep keys to Bruce, "Liz, have you got the keys to your car?"

Elizabeth nodded.

"Then let's get going," Nicholas said.

Elizabeth stared back uneasily at Jessica. Suddenly she realized that she had broken out in a cold sweat.

"See you later, Lizzie," Jessica said, struggling to make her voice sound natural.

Elizabeth felt like crying. Jessica called her Lizzie only when she was feeling unusually close to her sister.

Maybe it had just occurred to Jessica, too, how dangerous a situation they were walking into. Who knew when, or under what circumstances, she and Jessica would see each other again?

* * *

Arriving on the Densons' street, Bruce parked out of sight of the house. As he and Jessica sat waiting for Nicholas's first call, they went over their plan one last time. "I'll go in the side door," Bruce told Jessica, "to let the Morrows out. You just keep Mitch busy in the front of the house."

"How will I know you've rescued them?" Jessica asked. "I don't want to get stuck here when Mitch's father comes back."

Bruce thought for a second. "It'll be kind of obvious, won't it? When you see me charging for the Jeep with Mr. and Mrs. Morrow running after me, you'll know!"

"Come on," she begged him. "What if I'm looking the other way?"

Bruce shook his head. "Just keep Mitch busy," he ordered her. "I'll whistle when it's time for you to run to the Jeep. OK?"

"OK," Jessica said, feeling better.

Just then the phone rang in the Jeep. It was Nicholas. He and Elizabeth were at the Morrow plant, and everything looked fine so far. "I'll call back as soon as Claire and Regina show up," Nicholas said nervously.

"Good luck," Bruce said, hanging up the car phone.

He relayed the news to Jessica, and the two of them sat in tense silence, waiting for the phone to ring again. When it did, Jessica jumped; her nerves were getting frayed.

Bruce picked up the phone. "Hello?"

"They're here!" Nicholas whispered into the phone.

When Bruce hung up, he turned to Jessica. "Well, this is it. Let's go!"

Quickly and quietly, Bruce walked up the driveway as Jessica went to the door.

"Jessica!" Mitch gasped when he opened the door a minute later. "This really isn't a very good time," he told her.

Jessica frowned. "I thought we had a date," she said, trying to see past him into the house. As she'd hoped, Mitch came out onto the porch and closed the door.

"You mean the beach party," he said slowly. "Jessica, I really do have other plans. I don't want to be rude, but I—"

"What time is it?" Jessica demanded. "Is it seven o'clock yet? If you're busy, maybe I'll just go over to the beach party by myself."

Mitch glanced down at his watch. "It's just after seven," he told her. "Look, Jess, I'm sorry, but I—"

His voice broke off, and a terrible expression crossed his face. "Jessica, I really like you," he said rapidly, staring at the street. "And I don't want you to get hurt. So for your own good, would you please get out of here right away?"

Jessica spun around, following his gaze. For an instant her heart stood still.

Phillip Denson's light blue Dodge was barreling down the street toward the house. And a minute later, tires squealing, Denson drove up the side driveway, jumped out of the car, and started to walk into the house through the side door.

"Bruce!" Jessica screamed, pushing Mitch away and grabbing for the door.

"Get out!" Mitch hollered. "It isn't safe in there, Jessica. My father's got a gun!"

Jessica didn't even hear what Mitch was saying. All she knew was that Phillip Denson had just walked into the house, probably no more than a minute or two after Bruce. She had to get inside somehow.

"Stop it!" Mitch was yelling. He'd managed to get Jessica in a stronghold, pinning her arms behind her back. Squirming wasn't doing any good. He had her trapped.

Jessica knew she had to do something drastic. Everything depended on it. Squirming as far sideways as she could, she sank her teeth into the skin on Mitch's arm and bit down with all her might.

"Ow!" Mitch hollered, loosening his grip just long enough to let Jessica charge through the front door.

"Bruce!" she screamed, knocking over a little table and sending a lamp flying as she raced through the living room. "Mrs. Morrow, Mr. Morrow—"

But the cry died on her lips as Jessica saw the tangle of people racing toward her. Bruce was first, with the Morrows and Phil Denson in hot pursuit.

It was too late to turn back. She'd built up too much momentum. The next thing she knew, she had crashed straight into Bruce. Mitch, who was right behind her, had run into Mrs. Morrow.

Mrs. Morrow was sobbing; Denson was hollering; and all Jessica could concentrate on was Denson's gun, which was pointed at them!

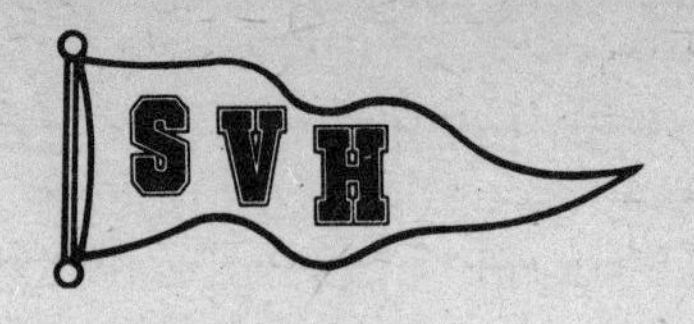

Eleven

"Don't move, any of you!" Denson growled, pointing his gun at the group and running his eyes meanly around the room. "Do you hear me? If one person moves, I'm going to start shooting."

Jessica shivered. She didn't like the look on Denson's face one bit.

Bruce was behind her, his hand pressing hard on her arm. "We've got to make a run for it," he whispered against her ear. "I'm going to try to block him. See if you can get to the Jeep."

"Shut up!" Denson yelled, pointing the gun directly at Jessica. "Didn't you hear what I said? No one moves in here—and no one talks, either!"

Jessica froze. The gun was pointing straight at her chest. She felt as though the air were pushing in on her. It hurt even to breathe, she was so scared.

"Leave her alone, Dad!" Mitch yelled. And to Jessica's disbelief, he lunged forward, knocking the gun out of his father's hand and sending him sprawling on the living room floor.

"Come on!" Bruce cried. "Let's go!" Grabbing Mrs. Morrow by the hand, he spun around. He charged through the front door and across the Densons' lawn to the street, where the Jeep was parked.

"Come on, Jessica," Mr. Morrow was urging, pulling at her arm. For a moment Jessica couldn't move. She felt as if she were glued to the floor. Mitch was kneeling over his father, tears running down his face. The next minute, Jessica had spun on her heel, racing after Bruce and the Morrows.

"You were so brave, both of you," Mr. Morrow said in a low voice, once they were all in the Jeep.

"Poor Mitch," Jessica said. "Do you think Denson will hurt him?"

"Not now," Mr. Morrow said grimly. "Right now, I think Denson's mind is on getting the chip prototype and the plans, covering his tracks, and getting out of the country."

"We've got to get to the plant right away," Bruce said, shifting gears on the Jeep and stepping on the gas pedal.

"I think," Mr. Morrow said, picking up the car phone, "we'd better call the police. Knowing

Denson, there's going to be a pretty nasty scene ahead of us at the plant."

"Regina!" Mrs. Morrow said brokenly, hiding her face in her hands.

"Anyway, I think we'd better get ourselves a little bit of help," he said grimly.

Jessica bit her lip, wondering how Nicholas and Elizabeth were right then. She'd been so relieved to have escaped from the Densons' house that she hadn't realized the most dangerous part of the rescue operation was still ahead of them. They still had to make sure Denson didn't steal the chip prototype; and somehow they had to get Regina away, unharmed, from Claire.

Jessica's heart began to pound rapidly. "I hope they're all OK," she whispered to Bruce. She had never felt so frightened in her life.

"OK," Elizabeth called softly to Nicholas. "I think they're coming out of the factory now. Yes—there they are! Are you ready to call the police?"

"I'm ready," Nicholas called back, his voice thick with anxiety. "What's happening now, Liz? I can't see a thing behind these damn bushes!"

"It looks like . . ." Elizabeth squinted, trying to see what was going on. "There are three people," she said at last. "Regina, Claire, and some man. He looks like he's about fifty years old, with gray hair," she reported.

"That must be Walter," Nicholas said, trying hard to get a look. "What's happening now?"

"Well, they're shaking hands. It looks like Walter is giving Regina a package."

Nicholas gasped. "The chip prototype!"

"He's turning around now," Elizabeth continued. "He's going back into the building. Nicholas, they're starting down the main driveway. This is it!"

"Be careful," Nicholas said, his dark eyes filling with emotion.

"I will be," Elizabeth promised, getting to her feet. Her legs felt cramped from kneeling so long.

"And, Liz . . ." Nicholas began, his voice trembling.

Elizabeth looked at him quizzically.

"Whatever happens, I just want you to know how grateful I am to you and Jessica for being so brave for my family's sake," he whispered emotionally.

"It's all going to be OK," Elizabeth told him. Her heart pounding, she slipped out from her hiding place behind the bushes and began walking toward the security gate—and toward Regina and Claire Davis.

Nicholas had managed to get a security tag for Elizabeth so she could get past the security booth. She still had no idea what would be the best way to stall Claire while Nicholas called the police. Now, seeing the woman coming toward her, Elizabeth realized what an enormous risk she was taking. Claire probably had a gun in her handbag. What if she took it out?

Elizabeth was counting on the fact that Claire would be afraid to arouse the suspicions of the guard.

"Excuse me!" Elizabeth called as she got closer to her friend and the older woman. She had never thought so quickly in her entire life. "I'm a reporter from the *Sweet Valley News,* and I'm trying to get access to the plant to ask the foreman a couple of questions. Do either of you know the foreman here?" she continued, keeping her face straight as she looked from Claire to Regina.

Regina stared at Elizabeth as if she were mad. But she managed to keep her composure. Her fingers were trembling, Elizabeth noticed. Other than that, she looked cool and collected.

Claire, on the other hand, was glaring at Elizabeth. An instant later a strange expression crossed her face. "Don't I know you from somewhere?" she asked, irritated. "Weren't you the one who came by the house looking for Regina last week?"

Elizabeth thought fast. Her one aim was to detain Claire. The sooner the woman suspected what she was trying to do, the harder her job would be.

"Oh, no," Elizabeth said, laughing merrily.

"You must mean my twin sister, Jessica. I don't know Regina Morrow myself," she lied, turning with a quizzical smile to her friend. "Are you Regina, by any chance? Maybe you could help me. Do you know any of the foremen here?"

Claire was staring at Elizabeth, her gray eyes narrowing. "We don't have time to stand around talking nonsense," she snapped, grabbing Regina roughly by the arm. "Do we, dear?" she added, stepping sideways around Elizabeth and pulling Regina with her.

"What about the guard?" Elizabeth said quickly, turning to point at the man. "Would he be helpful?"

"We really *don't* have time for this," Claire sputtered, marching forward with Regina, who looked helplessly back at Elizabeth, her blue eyes filling with tears.

Oh, no, Elizabeth thought helplessly. The way things were going, she might just have to take Jessica's advice after all and pretend to trip in front of Claire!

"Look," she said desperately, hoping Nicholas had contacted the police, "can I at least ask you a question or two about the way computers are infiltrating every home and business?"

"I don't know anything about that," Claire snapped, turning away.

But the few minutes that Elizabeth had managed to stall Claire had already made a big difference. She could tell from Claire's irritation that it had occurred to her that something strange was going on but that there wasn't anything she could do about it. She was afraid to make a scene, so she had to put up with Elizabeth's irksome questions.

Meanwhile, Nicholas was arguing furiously with Sergeant O'Brien from the pay phone. "This *isn't* a crank call," he said, wiping his brow. He couldn't believe this! The officer seemed to be having a hard time believing that Regina was really in trouble.

"I don't know," Sergeant O'Brien said dubiously. "Some girl called us up last week about something funny going on up at the Morrow place. When we drove over there, everything was in perfect order. Now you're telling me—"

"This is Nicholas Morrow," Nicholas fumed. "My parents have been kidnapped, and so has my sister. We're at the MicroTech plant out on Route Five right now, and my sister's life is in danger. If you don't get some squad cars out here right away—"

"Just a minute, son," Sergeant O'Brien said. "I've got another call."

Nicholas was practically sputtering with rage. This was unbelievable, he thought. He couldn't see Elizabeth from the phone booth, but he was sure she wouldn't be able to stall Claire much longer. The police *had* to believe him, they just had to!

"Are you still there?" Sergeant O'Brien's voice boomed through the receiver.

"Yes, sir," Nicholas said miserably.

"I just got a call from your father," Sergeant O'Brien told him. "He confirmed the entire story. He's on his way to the plant right now, and we're going to meet you both there with every squad car we can get."

Nicholas didn't bother to answer. He could hear the officer's voice spluttering from the receiver as he dropped it and raced forward to meet Elizabeth. Claire Davis was walking forward with Regina, her face red with anger. Elizabeth was hurrying after them, a desperate expression on her face.

Charging forward, Nicholas grabbed his sister by the arm.

"Nicholas!" Regina cried, bursting into tears.

"Let go of her," Claire said harshly, putting her hand on her purse. "I've got a gun. If you don't let go of her right now, I'll fire!"

Elizabeth felt a cold sweat breaking out on her brow. She had never been so frightened in her life. Where were the police? she was thinking desperately. If only there were some way of getting the security guard's attention. But as she turned her head toward the security box, Elizabeth realized with horror that the guard was walking toward the plant, presumably to begin locking up. There was no way of attracting his attention without alerting Claire Davis.

The next thing she knew, the silence was broken as the sound of squealing tires pierced the air. Bruce, Jessica, and the Morrows, in the Jeep, were driving at breakneck speed toward the plant!

An instant later Bruce had slammed on the brakes, and everyone spilled out of the Jeep. "Mom!" Regina screamed, breaking free from Claire Davis and stumbling forward. "Daddy!"

"Everyone freeze!" Claire cried, pulling a silver pistol out of her handbag. Elizabeth grabbed onto Nicholas's arm for support.

She couldn't believe her eyes. Phillip Denson's car was only a few seconds behind Nicholas's Jeep. Mitch was beside him in the car. Pulling the Dodge up fast in a cloud of dust, Denson leaped out of the driver's seat. His son got out of the passenger side, and followed slowly behind. Denson pointed his gun at the group gathered at the front gates of the plant.

We're in for it now, Elizabeth thought, hanging on to Nicholas's arm for dear life.

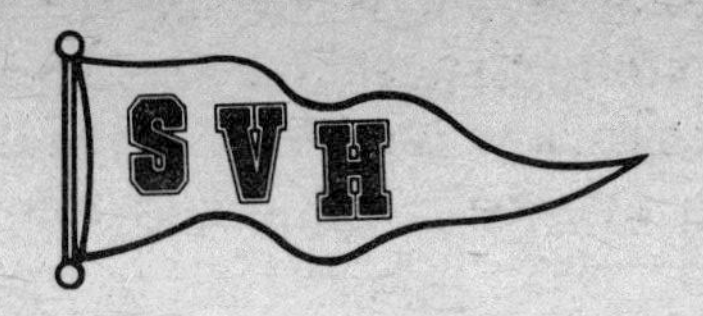

Twelve

For several seconds no one moved. Then Mr. Morrow spoke, his voice quavering.

"Phil, what is it you want? I mean, *really* want?"

Squaring his shoulders and wiping one hand on his shirt, Phillip Denson faced his former employer. "I want to make you suffer," he said evenly, his eyes narrow and mean. Mitch, who had gotten out of the car a minute after his father, was staring sheepishly at the ground, obviously wishing he were somewhere far away. "I want you to suffer for having me arrested five years ago."

"We've already been through this, Phil," Mr. Morrow said, sounding tired. "I had to prosecute you. You were embezzling funds from the company."

"That was your story!" Denson snorted derisively. "Hell," he added, wiping his perspiring face on his shirt-sleeve, "maybe I did take that money. But you didn't have to ruin my whole life, Morrow."

"You got what you deserved," Mr. Morrow said calmly. "You should have thought of the consequences when you stole that money."

"What I deserved?" Denson repeated, shaking his head. "When I got out of jail last year, I couldn't get another job in the computer field. No one would hire me. My wife had left me, so it was just Mitch and me. Not a very comfortable situation."

"What do you want?" Mr. Morrow repeated roughly. "You've made all of us suffer enough now as it is. Is it the chip prototype you really want?"

Phillip Denson laughed. It was a horrible, mean kind of laugh that made shivers run up and down Elizabeth's spine. "That's only the beginning," he answered, taking the package from Regina. "This little box here is going to make my fortune when I get to Rio. But," he added, gesturing at Mr. Morrow with the gun, "it wouldn't be very wise for me to leave town with so much unfinished business here, would it?"

"What are you saying?" Nicholas interrupted, his green eyes flashing.

Phillip Denson jerked his gun in Nicholas's direction. "Keep your mouth shut," he said harshly. "You'll find out what I'm saying when I'm good and ready for you to find out."

Jessica burst into tears. "Are you going to shoot us all?" she demanded, her face streaked with dust.

Denson didn't answer, and the terrible silence following Jessica's question was suddenly shattered by the sound of sirens in the distance. "What's that?" Denson asked sharply, looking around him in alarm. As if on cue, Nicholas and Bruce jumped on Phillip Denson from opposite directions, knocking the gun out of his hand and trying to pin him to the ground.

"Let him go!" Claire screamed, aiming her gun at Nicholas and pulling the trigger. There was a loud explosion as the gun went off.

Jessica closed her eyes and screamed at the top of her lungs.

At first Elizabeth couldn't tell what had happened. Nicholas and Bruce were still scrambling around on the ground with Denson, and Claire had fallen to her knees, sobbing, the pistol smoking in her hands. Her shot had missed Nicholas by inches.

"Everyone freeze!" an unfamiliar voice shouted, and when Elizabeth looked up again, she couldn't believe her eyes. Six policemen, all armed, were running toward them.

"Put your hands up, Denson!" one of the officers cried, moving forward with a gun in his hand.

Phillip Denson staggered to his feet and put his hands in the air. His gun lay a few feet away on the ground.

"Get the cuffs on him," the officer said to a policeman standing near him. "And the woman, too," he added, as one of the men pulled Claire Davis to her feet.

Within seconds Phillip Denson, Claire Davis, and Mitch were against the side of the police car, being frisked before being taken down to the station. "I just want you to know right now that you have the right to remain silent. Anything you say can be used against you in a court of law. You have the right to the presence of an attorney. If you cannot afford an attorney, one will be appointed for you prior to questioning, if you so desire."

"Anything I've got to say can be said right now," Phillip Denson growled. "I'm not sorry about anything I've done. Does everyone hear that?" Claire Davis remained silent.

Regina had run over to her parents and Nicholas the minute the handcuffs were snapped around Phillip Denson's wrists. The four of them were hugging one another and laughing and crying at the same time.

Jessica was standing apart, watching unhappily as the policeman led Mitch to the squad car. "I can't stand it," she told one of the officers. "It isn't fair, arresting Mitch! He saved my life. In fact, he probably saved *all* our lives!"

"We have to take him down to the station now," the officer said gently. "But if Mitch is innocent, nothing will happen to him."

"I can't believe it," Nicholas said, walking over to Elizabeth. "We actually managed to pull this crazy thing off! We actually *did* it!" The next thing Elizabeth knew, Nicholas had grabbed her around the waist and started to dance around with her in excitement.

But Elizabeth couldn't feel jubilant yet. Before Nicholas hugged her, she had witnessed one of the most moving sights she had ever seen.

Regina, her eyes filled with tears, had turned from her parents to put her arms around Bruce Patman. And the two had held each other lovingly—as if they'd never, ever let each other go again, not as long as they lived!

It was dark by the time Nicholas's Jeep and the twins' Fiat pulled up the long driveway to the Morrows' mansion. After a good deal of debate and discussion, the twins had decided it was time to confess everything to their parents. Elizabeth was the one who finally had to do the talking. She had called their parents from the police station, filling them in on everything that had happened and trying to calm them down when the Wakefields realized the danger the twins had been in. Finally all was calm again, and Elizabeth asked if they could join the

Morrows for a celebration dinner before coming home. Everyone agreed it would be much more fun to stop at Guido's Pizza Palace and get takeout pies instead of going to a restaurant.

"I don't know about anyone else," Mr. Morrow said happily, "but I just want to get back to my own dining room table!"

Minutes after they arrived, the Morrow house was blazing with lights. The smell of pizza wafted invitingly from the kitchen, and Nicholas ran from room to room, opening windows to let the warm sea breeze fill the house.

"God, it feels good to be home!" he cried, looking around him, joy in his eyes.

"Thanks a lot," Bruce said dryly. "Didn't you like living in bachelor simplicity over at my place these past few days?"

Nicholas laughed. "There's no place like home, Bruce," he teased. "There's just no place like home."

After dinner Mr. and Mrs. Morrow collapsed on the couch and looked around them with a mixture of delight and disbelief. "I don't know who to thank first," Mr. Morrow said warmly, looking at the twins and Bruce. "You were all amazing! How did you ever come up with that brilliant rescue scheme?"

Piece by piece, the four heroes recounted the adventures of the last week. "But it was easy for us," Jessica reminded the Morrows. "It was you guys who were the *real* heroes. Every time I thought of Regina here, all by herself . . ."

Bruce hugged Regina warmly. "It made me furious," he told her, kissing her on the tip of her nose. "Absolutely furious."

"I can't believe we're all here, safe and sound." Mrs. Morrow sighed. "Regina, come sit next to me for a minute," she pleaded, patting the couch beside her.

Regina turned, a smile on her face, and sat down beside her mother, entwining her fingers with her mother's. Suddenly Elizabeth realized what had only registered unconsciously before. Regina could hear!

"You know what I want to do once we've all had a few days to recover?" Mrs. Morrow asked. "I want to have the biggest, most spectacular party that this neighborhood has ever seen! It'll be a combination homecoming party for you and thank-you party for our four detectives," she continued, smiling. "How does that sound to all of you?"

"We have so much to celebrate," Regina said in a low voice. "Our reunion, first of all. And that we have good friends, who were willing to risk their lives to save us."

"Not to mention," Bruce said tenderly, "the fact that a certain very brave young lady now has eighty-five percent normal hearing!"

Jessica gasped. "Regina, does that mean you'll

be able to stay in Sweet Valley? You won't have to go back to Switzerland?"

Regina shuddered. "I don't ever want to be separated from my friends and family again," she said fervently.

"Well, according to Dr. Friederich, you won't have to be," her father announced. "That was one of the reasons why your mother and I were coming to Switzerland, Regina. We wanted to tell you in person. Dr. Friederich sent us a letter and enclosed your most recent medical files. He thinks that the final round of treatments can be done on an out-patient basis in Los Angeles."

A cry of joy went up around the room.

"This really does call for a party," Bruce declared happily. "Mrs. Morrow, is there some way I can help? I want this to be the biggest, noisiest, most fun party Sweet Valley has had in years!"

"Just come and enjoy yourselves." Mrs. Morrow laughed and hugged Regina close to her. "You've all done enough as it is. Let's make the party this Friday night," she added. "Is that OK with you, Kurt?"

Mr. Morrow laughed. "Friday night it is," he declared, hurrying over to the bar and taking a bottle of champagne out of the minirefrigerator. "But for now, I think a toast is in order."

A few minutes later everyone had a chilled glass of champagne in his or her hand, and Mr. Morrow began the toast, lifting his glass to

Regina. "To my daughter," he said, his voice thick with emotion.

"To the best family in the whole world," Regina whispered, her eyes shining with tears. "And to the best friends anyone could ever have," she added, looking from Bruce to Elizabeth to Jessica.

"I'll drink to that!" Elizabeth and Jessica cried in unison, linking arms.

They could hardly believe it—the terrible ordeal was over at last!

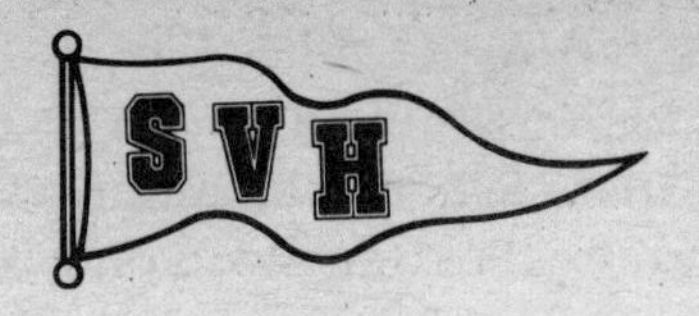

Thirteen

"I don't know," Jessica said, looking at herself critically in the full-length mirror in Elizabeth's room. "Don't you think this outfit's a little too ordinary?"

Elizabeth burst out laughing. "If there's one thing that outfit isn't," she declared, "it's ordinary!" Jessica was wearing a black leather miniskirt and a white T-shirt, the short sleeves rolled up. She had two clips in her hair that looked as though they should be holding loose-leaf notebook paper, and a brand new pair of sandals. Actually Elizabeth had to admit her twin looked good. She herself wouldn't be caught dead in an outfit like that, but it suited Jessica perfectly.

The twins were getting ready for the party at the Morrow estate. Lila Fowler, a friend of Jessica's, who Elizabeth thought was a snob, was picking them up. Most of the twins' friends would be at the party that night. It seemed that all week the talk at school had been about little other than the Morrow kidnapping. News had spread rapidly, and before long people were stopping Elizabeth and Jessica in the halls to ask questions about the kidnappers or hear more news about Regina.

"When's Regina starting school again?" Jessica asked, leaning over to fasten her earrings. "Everyone I see keeps asking me how long it'll be before she's back."

Elizabeth ran a comb through her silky hair, checking her reflection in the mirror over her dresser. "Mrs. Morrow thought she needed this week to rest, but as far as I know, she should be back on Monday," Elizabeth replied. "It's hard to believe she can really hear us now. You know what I mean?"

Jessica laughed. "I keep forgetting. I feel like she still has to read my lips."

Elizabeth's expression was thoughtful. "I still get upset every time I think about Phillip Denson and Claire Davis. What do you suppose the trial will be like?"

"Daddy seems to think Denson will get a long sentence," Jessica said. "He's not sure how long Claire Davis will get, though. Thank goodness they let Mitch off. I was really scared for him!"

"Well, he has you to thank for that," Elizabeth reminded her. "If you hadn't argued so persuasively for him, who knows what the outcome would've been?"

Jessica rearranged one of the clips in her hair. "Yeah," she admitted, "I guess I did him a favor. But the poor guy didn't even know half the story. And his father forced him to take part in the whole thing!"

Mitch, it turned out, had been told by his father and Claire Davis that the MicroTech chip was their own design. That was why they were stealing it, they told him, because it rightfully belonged to them!

Apparently Mitch had begun to be suspicious as soon as the Morrows were brought to the house. At that point, though, his father forced him to keep quiet and go along with everything he said. Once Mitch had tried to call the police, but his father had threatened to shoot him if he made another attempt.

Once the police were convinced Mitch really hadn't been involved—and that he'd actually saved Jessica's life by knocking his father down—they had dropped charges against him.

"So what's Mitch going to do?" Elizabeth asked, peeking out the window to see if Lila's car was anywhere in sight.

"He's moving to New Jersey," Jessica replied. "He's got an aunt out there who's supposedly really nice, very loving."

"That'll be a change." Unable to resist a chance to tease her sister, Elizabeth added slyly,

"I bet he's heartbroken. New Jersey's pretty far away from Sweet Valley, not like Fort Carroll!"

Jessica bit her lip. "It's probably just as well."

"Why?" Elizabeth demanded. "Don't tell me you've lost interest in the poor guy already."

Jessica laughed. "As I said, it's probably just as well. I wouldn't want Mitch to start being sorry he saved my life, would I? Anyway, I really want to forget all about the Densons for tonight. Don't you agree?"

"Hey, there's Lila!" Elizabeth exclaimed, hurrying over to the bed and grabbing her shoulder bag. "Come on, Jess, I don't want to miss a single minute of this party!"

"Jess, what in the world are you wearing?" Lila demanded as the twins got into her car. "You look like a member of the band, not a guest at the party!"

"You don't know anything about fashion," Jessica retorted. "As a matter of fact, I really like this kind of look."

Lila raised one eyebrow as she backed her car out of the driveway. "I sure hope this party is better than most of the ones I've been to lately. I'm getting sick of the high school crowd."

Jessica laughed. "From the few college friends you've introduced me to, I don't see that there's much difference, Lila."

Lila tossed back her long, light-brown hair.

"High school parties are so unsophisticated," she complained. "Except mine of course," she added. "You've got to admit I'm right. You two will probably be the toast of the party tonight," Lila continued. "Everyone's talking about how heroic you both are. It's positively *irritating*."

"Don't worry, Lila," Elizabeth reassured her. "People will probably forget all about it in a day or two."

"That's a day or two longer than I can stand," Lila remarked. "I'm just kidding," she added, sensing that Jessica had had just about enough. "Actually, I think you guys were both amazing. I'd never have been that brave in a million years."

Jessica laughed. "Too true, my friend," she said, searching for a good radio station.

"Cut it out, you two," Elizabeth admonished. She was used to bickering between her sister and Lila Fowler, but that night she didn't want anything to spoil her mood.

"Yeah, cut it out." Lila laughed and turned off her radio just as one of Jessica's favorite songs came blasting out of the speakers. "I've got some really good gossip for your 'Eyes and Ears' column, Liz."

"Good," Elizabeth said. "I've been so wrapped up with the Morrows that I haven't heard any juicy gossip in ages!"

Elizabeth wrote the gossip column for *The Oracle*, the Sweet Valley High newspaper, and she'd been hoping to get some interesting pieces of news at the party that night. But from Lila's excited tone, it sounded as if Elizabeth wouldn't have to wait long.

"Get a load of this for the oddest couple of the year," Lila said, and giggled. "Suzanne Hanlon and Ken Matthews. Isn't that a weird combination?"

Elizabeth couldn't believe she'd heard right. "Ken and Suzanne Hanlon?" she repeated, mystified. "Are you sure?"

"Absolutely," Lila said, looking smug. "It's been all over school. Supposedly she's completely reforming him. She's making him 'cultured.' " Lila burst out laughing as she slowed for a red light.

"I wonder if she's helping him out with his English," Elizabeth said thoughtfully.

"Well," Lila said conspiratorily, "I wasn't going to bring that up, since I simply *hate* spreading dirt around about people I like."

"Ha!" Jessica interjected.

"But," Lila went on, ignoring Jessica, "rumor has it that Ken's guidance counselor has laid down the law. Either he gets a B on his next English paper or he quits the football team. No ifs, ands, or buts."

"Wow," Jessica said. "That's pretty harsh."

Lila shrugged. "Maybe Suzanne can help him out. She's supposed to be such a hotshot student. Anyway, I don't think it'll last. They're like oil and water. They'll never mix."

Elizabeth was thoughtful. "How well do you know Suzanne?"

"Not very well," Lila said, turning her car into the Morrows' driveway, "but I suppose if I feel like it, tonight's as good a time as any to get to know her better!"

"Yes," Elizabeth said, deep in thought. "Yes, Lila, I suppose you're right!"

Elizabeth couldn't remember a party that had been so much fun. The Morrows had transformed their enormous back lawn, setting up dozens of little tables with candles glowing on them. A large platform had been constructed near the house for dancing, with a hot rock band from San Francisco playing nearby. A buffet stocked with dozens of varieties of cocktail snacks and cold drinks extended across the patio.

"This is so wonderful," Elizabeth said to Mrs. Morrow as they stood out on a balcony, from which they had a perfect view of the party. She gave Mrs. Morrow an impulsive hug. "I don't know how you found the time after everything you've been through!"

"Regina helped me," Mrs. Morrow said, smiling lovingly at her daughter, who had just walked out on the balcony. "That made all the difference. Next week, when she's back at school, I'll be lost!"

But it was clear from the look on Skye Morrow's face that she was overjoyed that her daughter would soon be back at Sweet Valley High. And Bruce, coming up to Regina, looked happier than ever.

"Do you think I could steal away the guest of honor for one quick dance?" Bruce asked Mrs. Morrow, putting his arm around Regina.

Mrs. Morrow laughed. "Run along, you two," she told them.

Regina slipped her arm through Bruce's. "This time I won't have any excuse when I step on your feet," she told him. "I can actually hear the music tonight!" She and Bruce went inside.

Lingering behind on the balcony after Mrs. Morrow had excused herself to mingle with the other guests, Elizabeth watched Bruce and Regina and smiled fondly as they reappeared below a few minutes later. It was such a beautiful night. The moon looked like a silver pendant between the trees, and a soft, balmy breeze was moving gently across the lawn.

Elizabeth treasured moments like this. It felt wonderful to be there, to listen to the music, to look out at the swaying couples. So many of her friends were there, and she was looking forward to joining them soon. But she was also savoring this moment of privacy.

Suddenly her peaceful moment was shattered.

She could hear voices below her—and after the first few words of the conversation, she couldn't resist listening.

"Ken just *adores* classical music," a feminine voice was saying. "Don't you, Ken?"

Ken! Elizabeth's ears pricked up.

"I'm sorry, Suzanne," Ken said. "But I really don't know if I—"

"Oh, he's just so modest," the girl insisted.

Elizabeth leaned over the edge of the balcony for a closer look. Sure enough, Suzanne was holding forth in front of a small group of people, her arm tucked possessively through Ken's. To Elizabeth, Ken looked half enchanted and half miserable. It was hard to tell which emotion was stronger.

"We're getting season tickets to the symphony from my father," Suzanne was going on. "And Ken's so interested in poetry, too. He completely disproves the theory that football players can't be cultured, too."

Ken hung his head, not saying a word.

"Gee, Ken," one of the crowd remarked, "you think all that culture is going to help us win the big game against Palisades?"

Ken didn't answer.

"Oh, who cares about that?" Suzanne said sharply, holding Ken's arm more tightly. "Come on," she added. "Let's get some punch."

A brief silence followed, and Elizabeth

watched in amazement as Suzanne pulled Ken along with her.

Elizabeth frowned. She hadn't liked Suzanne's tone of voice at all. She had to admit Lila had a point. Ken and Suzanne didn't seem to make a very good pair.

I just hope Ken knows what he's getting into, Elizabeth thought, stepping back to join a circle of friends on the patio.

The Ken Matthews *she* knew certainly didn't prefer classical music and poetry to football! She just hoped Ken wasn't in for a complete rehabilitation from the very opinionated Suzanne Hanlon.

Poor Ken. Elizabeth sighed as she walked inside the house. He was failing English, facing getting kicked off the team—and apparently in for a crash course in culture from Hands-Off Hanlon herself!

***Will Suzanne succeed in changing Ken? Find out in Sweet Valley High #27,* LOVESTRUCK.**